dangerous
STRANGER

book four of the beautiful entourage series

E. L. TODD

This is a work of fiction. All the characters and events portrayed in this novel are fictitious or used fictitiously. All rights reserved. No part of this book may be reproduced in any form or by any electronic or mechanical means, including information storage and retrieval systems, without written permission from the publisher or author, except in the case of a reviewer, who may quote brief passages in a review.

Fallen Publishing

Dangerous Stranger

Cover Design provided by Dinoman Designs

Copyright © 2015 by E. L. Todd

All Rights Reserved

ISBN-13: 978-1511910798

ISBN-10: 1511910798

Jett & Ophelia

Jett

I plopped down in front of Danielle's desk and downed my beer.

She eyed me from her place in front of her computer. "You're really going to drink in here?"

"Why wouldn't I drink in here?" I took another drink.

"Because it's your office. A client could walk in any moment."

I shrugged and finished half of it. "You know, I've always thought you and I had something special." I tapped the surface of her desk with my knuckles. "Why don't we find out?"

She rolled her eyes dramatically. "I'm so sick of you guys hitting on me all the time."

"I'm so sick of you being so beautiful all the time."

She threw a pencil at me. "Knock it off. I know you just do it to get a rise out of me."

"You sure get a *rise* out of me."

She threw another pencil at me.

"Hey, watch the face!"

She opened her desk and pulled out a folder. "I have a new client for you. Don't act like this and you should be good." She tossed it in front of me.

I rolled my head around my shoulders, getting the kinks out. Then I cracked my knuckles and stretched my arms. It was a routine I did every time I got a new assignment. Then I opened it and took a look.

Danielle watched me. "Long story short, he's gay and his parents aren't exactly accepting of the practice. He thinks if he can have a professional by his side, he can make a good impression and get their acceptance. Nothing you haven't done before."

"This will be a walk in the park."

She gave me a teasing look. "Don't let another slip-up happen…"

I slammed the folder shut. "Let it go. It happened one time."

"And we were almost shut down," she hissed.

"Cato was fucking around with his client," I argued.

"But his client didn't sue us!" She threw another pencil at me.

"Okay, knock it off with the throwing missiles!" I threw them on the ground.

"Stop being annoying and I might consider it."

I turned back to the folder. "Anything important I should know?"

"His parents are wealthy. That's about it."

"When am I meeting him?"

"Tomorrow."

I nodded. "What's his name?"

"Maximillion."

"Pretentious name…I'm calling him Max. I can actually stomach that."

"Whatever, Jett. Call him whatever you want as long as you get out of my office."

I gave her my best smolder. "You're cute when you're angry."

She grabbed a handful of pencils out of her drawer in preparation to toss them at me.

"I get it," I said as I quickly got to my feet. "I'm out of here."

She chucked them at me just as I slipped out the door. "Asshole!"

***

Maximillion was sitting outside of Starbucks at a table with an umbrella hanging overhead. He wore a black t-shirt that was tight on his body and dark jeans. Just from looking at him, I wouldn't have known he was gay. He had fair skin and bright green eyes. His body was thick and toned like he hit the gym often. He was definitely a good-looking guy.

"Maximillion?" I asked.

He stood up and extended his hand to shake mine. "Yes. How are you?"

"Well. I'm Jett."

"Cool name." He dropped his hand and returned to his seat.

I sat down across from him. "First thing first, I'm not gay."

A smile stretched his lips. "Your personal life is none of my business and I wasn't going to ask. But I can tell you're straight from a mile away."

"Glad we got that cleared up."

He chuckled. "I get the impression you've done this before and it didn't end well?"

"He said he was in love with me and he stalked me for an entire month." It wasn't funny. I got really fed up with it toward the end. I even threatened to beat the shit out of him.

He didn't laugh at this revelation. "Well, I'm pretty normal so we'll be fine."

"I sure hope so." I flipped through his folder. "What exactly do you want me to do?"

"My parents don't know I'm gay, actually."

I flipped through the pages again. "You gave us the impression that they do."

"Well, I know they aren't accepting to homosexuality in general. They've made rude comments about it in the past. They won't be supportive when I tell them. I thought if I did it with a upstanding guy who's good-looking, well-mannered, and polite then they would understand that gay relationships aren't much different than straight ones."

"I see," I said quietly. I might be the recipient of a hate crime. It wouldn't be my first time.

"What are you thinking?" he blurted.

"Am I in any immediate danger?" I rested one ankle on the opposite knee while I examined him.

"No. My parents may not like you but they would never lay a hand on you. That includes the rest of my family. Don't worry about it."

"Okay," I said, feeling relieved. "Does anyone in your family know the truth?"

"My sister. That's about it."

"I'm guessing she doesn't care?"

"No, she doesn't," he said. "It's nice to have the support of at least one person. But I couldn't really hide it from her since we live together."

That was odd. Why did a twenty-seven year old man live with his sister? "Why is that?"

"I'm in between jobs right now. She has an extra bedroom so she let me stay with her."

"That was nice of her." If my brother needed a place to crash, I'd throw him on the street.

"We've always been close, even before she knew I preferred men."

"Having at least one person on your side makes your army that much stronger."

"I suppose." He watched the people pass on the sidewalk while he rested his chin on his knuckles. His eyes glistened like emeralds.

"You just don't look gay," I blurted.

He turned back to me. "Maybe because gay people…look like regular people?" There was a teasing note to his voice.

"Most of the gay men I work with our flamboyant and eccentric. You're very different from that."

He shrugged. "I guess I'm more mellow."

I turned back to his folder. "Is there anything specific you want me to do?"

"Just stand by my side and take their heat. That's all."

"No kissing," I blurted. "It's a rule."

"That's fine." The corner of his lip upturned in a smile. "With all due respect, you aren't my type."

Not his type? What did that mean? "Not your type?"

"Yeah…so you don't have to worry about me checking you out, not that you aren't good-looking. So, relax."

"I wasn't not relaxed."

"Okay." Judging the look in his eyes, he didn't believe me.

Not his type? Everyone thought I was hot. He didn't?

"My parents invited my sis and I over for dinner on Friday. I wanted to break the news then. Can you make it?"

His question shattered my thoughts. "You're my client. Your needs are my priority."

"That was a fancy way of saying yes," he said with a light laugh.

"That's how we do it at Beautiful Entourage—fancy."

***

Max and I approached the townhouse.

"So, how do you want to play this out?" I asked as I walked with my hands in my pockets.

"I'll introduce you as a friend for now. Then I'll tell them the truth."

"Okay." This was his gig so I would do anything he wanted. "So, if I'm not your type why did you hire me?"

A grin stretched his lips. "I hurt your ego, didn't I?"

"No," I said quickly. "I'm just curious."

"You're a man most people find attractive. And attractiveness makes people more liked. I just thought you had the right look for this circumstance."

"If I'm not your preference, what is?"

He chuckled lightly. "You really don't like not being eye-candy."

"That's not what I said..."

"If you're straight what does it matter?" He watched my face as he said it.

"Just curious..."

Max faced forward again. "You're funny."

I didn't have time to continue the conversation because we arrived at the door.

Max knocked then winked at me. "Showtime."

For a guy that was about to tell his family he was gay, he seemed oddly calm. When I did this in the past, the guys were always nervous wrecks. Max possessed a confidence I hadn't seen in someone in a long time.

The door opened, and a woman I assumed was his mother answered, "Hey, Maximillion. You look handsome, like always." She pulled him into a hug and kissed him on each cheek.

"Thank you, Mother. You look beautiful too."

"Such a sweet boy." She rubbed his shoulder. "Who's this?" she said as she turned to me.

"This is my friend Jett," Max explained. "I hope you don't mind me bringing him along."

"Not at all." She hugged me fiercely, like she was my own mom. "Of course he's welcome. Any friend of Max's is a friend of ours."

"Thank you, Mrs. Vanna."

"Call me Victoria," she said quickly.

"Will do."

She escorted us into the house and into the living room. "Your son is here, Scott."

He rose from the couch and hugged Max. "That's my boy." He had a stark resemblance to his son. Even in his older age, he had the shine of someone in his youth. He was thin and in shape. His wife was the same.

"Hey, Dad." Max hugged him back. "This is my friend Jett."

Scott shook my hand. "It's a pleasure. Welcome."

"Thank you, sir. Your home is lovely." It was from the Victorian era, and clearly had been restored. I knew they had money if they could afford a place like this. So far, they were extremely nice. I found it hard to believe they would treat Max differently when they knew the truth.

"Thank you, dear," Victoria said. "We've been living here for decades. We love it."

"You should."

Max stayed by my side, our shoulders almost touching. "Where's Ophelia?"

"She's finishing her special baked potatoes in the kitchen," Victoria explained.

"I'll be there in a second!" A distinctly female shout came from the kitchen.

"Take your time," Max said. "I don't want to see you anyway."

"Go to hell," she shouted back.

I tried not to smirk. "You guys seem close…"

Max shrugged. "I tease her because it's my job."

"And he takes that very seriously," Scott said.

"It's my purpose," Max said.

A woman emerged from the kitchen area and came into the living room.

My heart skipped a beat when I saw her.

Her shoulder length brown hair had a slight curl at the ends. It framed her face and moved like it was weightless. It had a distinct shine to it when she was directly under a light.

Her green eyes stood out like emeralds, shining with their own light. They absorbed and reflected every source of energy nearby, burning bright like a fire in the middle of the wilderness. They were so startling green I wasn't sure if they were real. They expressed her emotions like a beacon. When she was excited, they glowed.

She was short, perhaps five foot four, but she had legs that made her look six feet tall. Her dress reached slightly passed her thighs, and I could see the tone muscles of her thighs and calves. They were slightly tan, like she spent a lot of time outdoors. Heels were on her feet, and that gave her some more height.

Her curves were outlined in her tight dress. Her waist had a noticeable hourglass figure. Her hips were wide and her stomach was tight. Her chest was curvy and perky. That held my attention for several seconds before I moved onto her rounded shoulders.

My god, she was perfect.

I didn't even realize she was talking to me until Max nudged me in the side. "Sorry?"

Ophelia narrowed her eyes at me like she thought I was crazy, but there was a smile on her lips. Her eyes lightened like she was amused. "I said it's nice to meet you."

"Oh." It still took me a second to come back to earth. "Yeah, you too."

She held her hand out for me to shake.

I stared at it blankly.

Max discreetly nudged me in the side again.

"Oh yeah," I blurted. I shook her hand and gripped her tighter than I meant to. As soon as I felt her warm skin I didn't want to let go. I wanted to feel those hands all over me. I wanted her to grip my shoulders while she bounced on my dick and came all over me.

Whoa…where did that come from?

"It's nice to meet you," I said. "I'm…" I was drawing a blank. What was my name again? Shit, all I could think about was Rhett. But I knew that wasn't my name.

"Jett," Max said for me. "His name is Jett."

"Yeah," I said as I continued to shake her hand. "That's my name." Our handshake had lasted a full minute and I knew I needed to pull away. But I just held her hand like a freak.

"Well, I'm glad you're here." She quickly pulled her hand away.

"Yeah…I am too." *God, why did I sound like such an idiot right now?*

Max narrowed his eyes at me and gave me a look that said, "Get your shit together, man."

Ophelia turned to her brother. "I'm glad you made a friend."

"I have tons of friends," he replied.

"Imaginary ones don't count," she teased. She turned to the kitchen. "Now let's eat. I'm starving."

"Good idea, dear," Victoria said.

They walked into the kitchen and left us behind.

Max turned to me, and there was a menacing look on his face. "My sister is off limits. Do you understand me?"

"I…I'm not into her." It was the worst lie I ever told.

"Don't fuck with me," he hissed. "Every guy friend I have has a thing for her. You think you're the first?"

No, not when she was that hot. "A little warning would have been nice."

"You really can't control yourself from drooling and acting like an idiot?"

"I've never had a problem before…" *Until now.*

"You're supposed to be gay. That's never going to work if you keep eye-fucking my sister."

"I'm sorry. Geez."

"Just don't do it again," he barked.

"Okay, calm down. She just caught me off guard is all."

"A guy like you must get more pussy than he can handle," he said with a growl. "My sister shouldn't faze you."

You would think. "You can stop repeating yourself. I got it."

Dangerous Stranger

He gave me one final threatening look before he walked into the kitchen. "You better get it."

***

Dinner was pleasant. His parents asked him about work and the new things going on in his life. Max said he was working for a bank as an assistant manager, but I knew that was a lie since he said he was between jobs.

His parents asked me about my life. I lied and went with the cover I used for every escort that I had. They seemed impressed with me. That was good. If they liked me, they might be more accepting of Max when he told them the truth about his sexuality.

My eyes kept moving to Ophelia by their own will. Whenever she would put a spoon in her mouth, I watched the way her lips parted and caught sight of her small tongue. Every move she made was fascinating to me. Her arms were thin and toned and I could tell she worked out often. And she didn't just run, but she also lifted weights. It was clear just by looking at her.

Her dress had a deep cut to it and I could faintly see the swell of her breasts at the very top. I imagined what her tits looked like, and I wondered how they would feel in my palm while I groped them.

Shit, I was hot for her.

Every time I tore my gaze away from her, it just moved back. I watched every little thing she did, from the way she ate to the way she sipped her wine. I kept having daydreams of fucking her on my bed. My sexual desire was running wild with me, and I couldn't control my dirty thoughts. I'd seen plenty of hot chicks, but Ophelia was in her own league. She had to be the sexiest chick I'd ever seen—hands down.

"Anything new with you, dear?" his mom asked.

Max turned to me and gave me a look that said. "Now is the time."

That forced my look from Ophelia and to his parents. But I was still thinking about her—in really dirty ways.

"Actually, yeah," he said. "I think now is the best time to discuss it."

"Did you get promoted?" Victoria asked.

She was way off. I turned to Ophelia and watched her stare at her brother. There was support in her eyes. She knew what was coming and she was ready for it.

"No," Max said simply. "It's about my personal life."

"Did you meet someone?" Victoria asked.

I really hoped this went over well. His parents seemed nice so I doubted they would turn on him.

Max rested his hand on mine on the table. I didn't pull away and turned to him.

Both of his parents watched us, and when the realization hit them, their eyes widened.

"I know this is going to come as a bit of a shock, but I'm gay." He said it simply and without emotion. There was no fear. It seemed like he didn't say anything at all. He kept his hand on mine. "And Jett is someone I really care about. He's my boyfriend, actually."

His parents were dead silent. I even heard crickets.

Two minutes of silence passed.

His mom sipped her wine.

His dad played with his fork but didn't take another bite.

It was awkward—extremely awkward.

Max kept his hand on mine, holding his ground.

Maybe I should say something. "I really care about your son and I respect him. He's one of the best men I know and I'm a very lucky man to have him." Perhaps that would make it better.

It was still silent. Neither one of them acknowledged me.

Ophelia spoke up. "I'm very happy for you, Max. I don't care who you love or how you live your life. You're still my brother, my family. You have my support no matter what." Then she glanced at her parents.

I watched Ophelia, growing more attracted to her. She stood up for her brother, and I found that innately sexy. When she moved her arm to pick up her drink or fork, her breasts jiggled slightly. My cock started to harden.

"I...we don't know what to say," his mom finally said. It was clear she wasn't happy. Mortified would be a better word to describe her reaction. She was appalled that her son loved other men.

His dad didn't say anything at all, and his silence was a good indicator of his support; it was non-existent.

His mom finally looked at her son. "Maybe this is a phase…"

"It's not," Max said immediately. "I've been this way for years. I'm tired of hiding who I am."

"Maybe you should talk to someone," his dad suggested. "A professional."

"There's nothing to talk about," Ophelia said. "He's gay and there's nothing wrong with being gay."

Fuck, now I wanted her more.

Max gave her a slight nod in gratitude.

"We just think you might be confused," Victoria said. "We all lose our way sometimes."

"I actually found my way," Max said with a strong voice.

"We're here for you," Scott said. "But you need to let us help you."

"I don't need help," Max said. "I need support and love. I will be gay whether you approve or not. If you want nothing to do with me, I accept that. But tell me now so I can stop wasting my time at this dinner table."

I admired Max for being so strong. Most of my gay clients fell into painful tears and hoped their parents would change their minds. They hardly ever did.

"Of course we don't want nothing to do with you," his mom said. "We just think this might…be temporary."

"It's not," Max said. "It's not."

"Have you been doing drugs?" his dad asked.

"No," Max snapped.

"Even marijuana?" his mom pressed.

Max rolled his eyes. "No. Knock it off. I'm gay because I'm gay. Period."

"I think it's great," Ophelia said.

"Thanks," Max said to her. Then he turned back to his parents. "Take all the time you need to accept it. I'm not expecting you to immediately take this in. But don't tell me there's something wrong with me. And don't expect this to be temporary. This is who I am. And I will be this way forever."

His parents fell into silence again.

I knew that was the only reaction he would get from them for the evening. They were too stunned to speak. This obviously was news they weren't expecting to receive. For a moment, I pitied them. But then I didn't.

"We should go," Max said. "And give you some time to think about it." He rose from his chair and I did the same.

When Ophelia stood up too, I was glad she would be leaving with us. Like a moth obsessed with a flame, I wanted to follow her anywhere she went. She had my attention, something that's never happened before.

Without saying goodbye, we left the house and walked up the street.

Ophelia immediately comforted her brother. "I'm proud of you."

"Yeah?" He put his arm around her shoulder.

I almost felt like I was intruding by watching their affection. They really were close.

"Of course I am," she said. "I know that was hard for you—even if you act like it wasn't."

"I've done easier things," he said with a light laugh.

"Do you think they'll come around?" she asked sadly.

"I really don't know," he said with a sigh. "But I hope so."

She put her arm around his waist. "For what it's worth, if they disown you as a son then I disown them as their daughter."

"I don't expect you to choose sides."

"Well, I am."

He kissed her forehead and kept walking.

They really *were* close. Now I understood why he threatened me like a guard dog. He really was protective of his sister. He would rip me to pieces if I got too close. Why did the hottest girl have to be completely unavailable? Her brother wouldn't let me near her. And she thought I was gay.

I didn't have a chance.

***

We entered her apartment in Manhattan. It was a nice place. The kitchen looked brand new with granite countertops and stainless steel appliances. The hard wood floor accented the bright colors of her furniture. Floor-to-ceiling windows comprised the living room, showing the skyline in the distance.

She was loaded.

I wondered what she did for a living. But then it hit me.

She must be a model.

With a body like that and a flawless face, she had to be a model or an actress. Maybe even a porn star.

"You have a really nice place," I said, trying not to stare at her too much.

"Thank you. I like it."

"And I like crashing rent free," Max said with a smile.

"Well, don't get too comfortable," she warned. "Because it may not always be rent free." She walked to the refrigerator then opened it with her back to us. "Beer?"

I got a great view of her ass. It was perky, tight, and lifted. The arch in her back was deep and noticeable. I'd take her from behind in a heartbeat. I shook my head when my thoughts turned steamy. I couldn't have her so I should stop thinking about her in that way. But it was out of my control. If a kid was stuck in a room with a cookie jar, no one would judge him for having sweets before dinner. So why should they judge me for having a permanent boner around the hottest woman in the fucking world.

"I'll take one," Max said.

"Me too," I said when I came back to the conversation. "Please."

She opened them then brought them to us. When she handed me the bottle, our fingers grazed each other. It might be a crazy thought, but I thought I felt a spark between us. The energy differences between us created a strong potential. And like lightning to the earth, it created a spark.

"Thank you," I said as I stared into her exquisite face. She was more beautiful up close. She had thick and full lips. I wanted to suck her bottom lip until it was raw and I wanted to glide my hand through that silky hair.

"Sure," she said with a quick smile. Then she handed Max a bottle.

He gave me a threatening look the entire time.

Shit, he knows.

We sat down on the couch together, and I made sure Max was between his sister and me. Maybe if there was some distance between us my hard-on would disappear and I would get my head out of the gutter.

"So, how did this happen?" she asked as she drank her own beer.

The fact she drank beer was a turn on in itself.

"We met a few months ago at a bar," Max explained. "It just happened, and here we are."

"That's great," she said. "I didn't have any idea you were gay until you told me."

Max shrugged. "I'm pretty quiet about it."

"Is Jett your first?" she asked.

I liked hearing her say my name.

"Yeah." He rested his hand on my thigh. "We're pretty great together."

"We are," I said in agreement.

"Well, you're welcome to come over whenever you want," Ophelia said to me. "I won't stand in the way of true love."

"Thanks…" *She really didn't notice me eye-fuck the shit out of her?*

She finished her beer and left it on the coffee table. "Well, I'm going to get ready for bed. I'm assuming you guys want to hit the sack too." She winked then walked into her bedroom.

"Yeah, probably," Max said.

"Goodnight," she said.

Max held his beer up. "Goodnight."

"It was nice meeting you," she said. "I suspect we'll be getting to know each other pretty well."
Unfortunately. "Yeah, I think so."

E. L. Todd

Ophelia

When I woke up the next morning, I brewed a pot of coffee then made pancakes. I turned on my iPod and listened to music while I cooked, needing something to listen to while I endlessly flipped the pancakes in the pan.

A hand touched my shoulder and I flinched at the unexpected affection. I yanked my ear buds out.

"Sorry," Jett said quickly. "I just wanted to say hi. Didn't mean to scare you." He stepped back and eyed the spatula in my hand. "And I hope you aren't going to beat me with that…"

I realized I looked like an ax murderer so I lowered the cooking utensil and released a laugh. "Sorry. I got carried away."

"It's okay." He eyed the pan. "Pancakes?"

"I hope you're hungry."

"Wow, you're the best roommate ever." He had a nice smile on his lips. His face was slightly scruffy from not shaving for a few days. I liked the rugged look, with a hard jaw line and broad shoulders. His blue eyes were bright, and it was the only soft feature he had. He towered over me at six feet, and his arms were the size of my legs.

My brother had good taste in men. "Well, not when I scream at him for leaving his razor in the bathroom or leaving his dirty dishes out. Then he says I'm a cleaning Nazi."

He chuckled. "You like your apartment clean. There's nothing wrong with that."

I liked gay guys. They were sensitive and understanding. "Tell him that."

He came closer to me then stood beside me. "How can I help, sweetheart?"

"Sweetheart?" I asked with a raised eyebrow.

"Yeah." A confident smile stretched his lips. "You supported Max when he needed it. And now you're making breakfast for him. If that doesn't make you a sweetheart, I don't know what does." His arm touched mine, and I could feel the warmth transmit into me. He smelled good, like distant cologne. He wore the same clothes he wore the night before, but he rocked it like the outfit was brand new. His powerful chest and narrow hips were obvious even through his clothes.

My cheeks stretched into a smile. "I think you're the sweetheart."

He continued to stare at me, his eyes bright. He leaned close to me, just a few inches away. If I didn't know he was gay, I would assume he was going to kiss me. "So, how can I help?" He glanced down at my lips then looked into my eyes.

My arms actually broke out in goose bumps. *Was a gay guy seriously charming me? I needed to get my head on straight.* "You can set the table."

"Then that's what I'll do." He pulled away, taking his smell and warmth, and placed everything on the kitchen table.

"Sleep well?" I asked as I finished the last batch of pancakes.

"Yes. Did you?"

"I had a hard time getting to sleep."

"Why?" he asked.

"I kept thinking about my parents…I hope they accept Max. It would break my heart if they didn't."

"They will," he said with confidence. "Give it time." He poured himself a cup of coffee then sat down.

After I finished the pancakes, I set the plate down then sat across from him.

"They smell amazing." He eyed them but didn't take one.

"You can eat," I said.

He eyed the bedroom. "I'm not sure if I should wait for Max…"

I waved his comment off. "He might sleep until two. You never know with him."

"In that case..." He put a few on his plate then dug in.

I did the same.

Jett snuck glances at me every few minutes, taking in my face before he looked away.

"What?" I asked.

"Nothing," he said quickly.

"You keep staring at me."

He flinched noticeably then played it off like he hadn't. "You have the same eyes as your brother."

"Yeah, it's one trait we share." I lathered my pancakes in syrup and scarfed them down.

He ate with perfect manners and kept his elbows off the table. I couldn't help but notice the size of his powerful body. He was exceptionally good-looking, the kind of guy I would talk to if I ran into him somewhere. I wouldn't pass up the opportunity to get to know him. *Why were hot guys always gay?*

"What do you do, Ophelia?" he asked. "Are you a model?"

"Model?" I asked. "Why would you ask that?"

"Well, your apartment doesn't look cheap. And you're beautiful." He said it while he looked into my eyes, like he wasn't ashamed of what he said.

He found me beautiful? I assumed I looked like a troll to him since he preferred men. But I appreciated the compliment anyway. "I work for a fashion magazine. I'm the assistant chief editor."

"Impressive," he said with a nod. "Good for you."

"I like it. Sometimes I get to keep the shoes from the ads."

"Even better," he said as he kept eating.

"So, you really like my brother, huh?"

He averted his gaze and concentrated on his food. "I do. He's a strong man that has confidence I'm immediately attracted to."

"He is pretty great," I agreed. "I've always looked up to him."

"It seems like he should be looking up to you," he said. "You're very successful, bright, and beautiful."

I tried not to smile. "You're the biggest ass-kisser I've ever met."

He stopped eating. "I'm not kissing your ass…"

I chuckled. "If Max likes you, then I like you. You don't need to try and impress me. Don't stress about it."

He returned to eating. "Your opinion does matter to me, but my compliments were genuine. But you must get sick of hearing them since you get those comments all the time."

"Not really," I said. "My brother tells me I look like a gremlin almost every day."

He laughed. "Sibling love."

"And I say he looks like a giant douchebag."

"Burn," he said. He finished his plate then touched his flat stomach. "That was delicious. Thank you."

"You're welcome."

Max came out of his bedroom with messy hair and sleepy eyes. "Morning." He stretched his arms over his head and yawned.

"Morning," I said. "There's food and coffee."

"Thank god." Max moved to me and gripped my shoulder. "Morning, babe."

Jett flinched at the touch, like he wasn't expecting it. Then he recovered. "Morning. Take a seat next to me." He pulled the chair out for him.

Max sat down then glanced between us. "What were you guys talking about?"

"How much of a kiss-ass he is," I said with a laugh.

Jett shrugged in omission. "She's exaggerating."

"I have a feeling she's not." He gave Jett an ominous look.

I'd never been around Max when he had a boyfriend so I wasn't sure how he would behave. They seemed to have a relationship based on friendship and jokes. It wasn't much different than a relationship between a man and a woman.

Max helped himself to the pancakes. "These are good."

"Thanks," I said. I looked at my watch. "I need to get going. But I'll see you later."

Sadness came into Jett's eyes. Or was that something else? "Thank you for breakfast."

"Anytime." I walked into my room, but before I closed the door I heard some of their conversation.

"Try anything and you're dead," Max said.

"I understand," Jett said. "You don't need to repeat yourself."

I had no idea what that meant, and I didn't ponder on it.

***

Cameron arrived at my office at noon to pick me up for lunch. "Ready to eat?" he asked as he knocked on the door.

"I'm starving," I said. "I only had pancakes for breakfast."

"Then let's get going." He stood in front of my desk with his hands in his pockets.

After I grabbed my purse, I gave him a quick kiss on the lips. "Where do you want to eat?"

"I don't care," he said, like always.

"I'm in the mood for Mediterranean. Is that okay?"

"Whatever you want." He held my hand as we left and walked up the sidewalk.

When we entered the restaurant, Cameron walked in first then headed to the table. I followed behind him then took a seat. Once we were sitting, he immediately looked at the menu and made his selection within seconds. Then he looked out the window like he was bored.

"How's your day going?" I asked.

"Fine. Pretty slow."

Cameron was a lawyer but it didn't seem like he cared much about his job. I'm not sure why he killed himself during school to do something he hated. But I didn't press him on it. He didn't ask how my day was going.

A blonde waitress approached our table. Her hair was in a braid over one shoulder, and she was extremely pretty. I liked the color of her eye shadow so I stared at it for a while, wondering where she got it from. "What can I get you guys?"

Cameron stared at her like she was an abstract painting. "Uh…what do you recommend?"

I cocked an eyebrow. He never asked that question.

"Our special of the day is our mahi mahi. Everyone seems to like it," she said with a smile.

"I'll take that," he said.

He didn't even like fish.

"And you?" she asked as she looked at me.

I looked at Cameron and saw him stare at her chest. "I'll have the chicken *breast*." The jab was directed at him.

"Great." She took our menus. "It'll be out soon." When she walked away, Cameron still stared at her. And I assumed he was staring at her ass.

"How would you feel if I checked out every cute guy that walked by?"

"Huh?" He turned to me, clearly not hearing a word I said because our waitress's ass was more important.

"Forget it." I looked out the window. I knew Cameron checked out other women and that didn't bother me. But to do it right in front of me, and with such enthusiasm was disrespectful.

He didn't make conversation with me. His eyes searched the restaurant.

"You don't even like fish."

He shrugged. "I'll give it another chance."

There were a lot of good things about Cameron, but when he pulled shit like this I forgot about them. "Since you're so interested in our waitress how about you go out with her instead of me?"

He sighed in irritation. "Not this again..."

"I'm being serious."

"You're always being serious," he said in a dark tone.

"I don't care that you check out other women just don't do it in front of me. It's not much to ask for."

"I wasn't checking her out," he argued.

Now I wanted to smack him. "More than anything, I hate lying. Be a man and own up to it."

"You need to chill out."

I was starting to boil. "You need to be a better boyfriend. We hardly see each other because we work so much. So when we are around each other, you should pay more attention to me and actually look at me, not the waitress's rack."

He rolled his eyes.

"Why are you such a pig?" I hated this side of myself. He brought it out of me and I loathed that fact. I was calm and reserved and it took a lot to make me mad. But Cameron had been pissing me off lately.

When we first started dating a long time ago, I was the only girl in the world who existed. He couldn't stop staring at me, and he wanted to know every detail of my day. Now he was more interested in waitresses and anything with a vagina. I knew relationships got stale as time wore on but I felt like he wasn't making an effort anymore.

I started to feel helpless, like Cameron didn't really care about me. But if that was how I really felt, why was I still in this relationship? I deserved more and I wouldn't put up with less. "Now that you're officially single, you can ask out Blondie." I snatched my purse then stormed out.

"Ophelia!" Cameron called after me.

I kept walking. I was sick of his shit. When I made it out of the restaurant, I felt a little better. I still had twenty minutes left on my lunch break, so I could grab a sandwich and head back to the office.

"Ophelia." Cameron chased me. "Don't be like this."

I turned around and pointed him in the chest. "I'm sick of the way you treat me. We used to be in love but now you just act like I'm a chore. If you're that entranced by another woman, then I'm obviously not enough to satisfy you. So let's just walk away from each other—for good. You used to hang onto every word I said, and I used to be the only girl in the room. Now I'm just some bitch that you can't stand. Well, that's fine. Have a good life." I walked away again.

"Don't be like this." He grabbed my wrist.

I twisted out of his grasp just as my brother taught me. Then I pushed him back. "If you really wanted me to stick around, you would have looked at me once at lunch. But you didn't." I gave him a final glare before I marched up the sidewalk.

This time, he wasn't stupid enough to follow me.

***

The second I walked through the door, I tossed my purse on the counter so hard it slid off the table and landed on the floor. Then I kicked my heels off, letting them fly in completely opposite directions. I threw the refrigerator door open and grabbed a beer. Then I downed it like water.

"Had a bad day…?" Max was sitting in the living room with his laptop on the coffee table.

I didn't even notice him. "You could say that."

"I can't even drink a beer that fast."

"What can I say?" I said coldly. "I'm a natural."

"Yeah…something is definitely wrong."

I crossed my arms over my chest and sighed. I wish I wasn't so worked up over Cameron. He wasn't worth the heartache.

Max patted the spot beside him on the couch. "Talk to me."

I grabbed another beer then sat down.

"Start from the beginning."

"No, I'll start at the end. I dumped Cameron."

Both of his eyebrows shot up. "Why?"

"Because he's a fucking dick. That's why."

"Give me more than that," he said calmly.

Just thinking about it pissed me off. "When we were at lunch today, he kept checking out the waitress. And not discreetly or quickly, but blatantly staring at her rack and her ass like I didn't exist. Then he ordered fish when he hates fish, just because she recommended it. When she was gone, all he did was search for her. It was like I didn't exist. He didn't even bother starting a conversation with me. We're so different than what we used to be. So, I stormed out and told him we were done. He tried to chase me but I threatened to emasculate him if he did."

Max nodded but didn't say anything.

"I hate him." I didn't mean it. But I was so mad I thought I did. All I wanted was for him to treat me the way he used to in the beginning of our relationship. I was his entire life. Now I was…I didn't even know what I was.

"You made the right decision," Max said calmly. "If you aren't happy, you shouldn't be in that relationship."

"I've never cared about him checking out other women. It doesn't bother me. But to do it in front of me…it was just…mean."

"It would bother anyone, Ophelia," he agreed. "But when people are in loving relationships, they don't check out other people."

"They don't?" I asked.

"Do you?"

When I thought about it, I realized I didn't. "No…"

"When you're in love, everyone else fades to the background. It's not rocket science to know someone is attractive, but to actively check them out is a different situation."

"Is that how you feel about Jett?" He was one of the most handsome men I'd ever seen. It was a shame to all the women in the world that he was gay.

"Yeah," he said after a pause. "Why would I check out other men when I have him?"

"Yeah…"

"I know you're my sister and I know I'm gay, but you're a beautiful woman, Ophelia. Even I will admit that. You're cool, like one of the guys, but you're also a strong, independent, and brave woman. Any guy would kill to have you. The fact Cameron doesn't appreciate you is a sign that the relationship is over—it's been over the moment he undervalued you."

My brother always made me feel better without even trying. "Thanks…"

"Of course." He patted my shoulder then dropped the embrace.

"You love this guy?" I asked.

"I do," he said with a nod.

"I'm so jealous. You guys are happy and in love…I can't get a guy to feel that way about me if I tried."

He shook his head. "You aren't the problem. You just haven't found the right guy."

Dangerous Stranger

Chapter 3

Jett

"I'm not kidding. This chick is the most beautiful fucking thing in the world."

River drank his beer with an incredulous look on his face. "That's a bold statement."

"I know it is," I said immediately. "And it's damn true."

"You got a picture?"

"No...that would be weird if I tried to get one."

He drank his beer then set it on the coaster. "Are you going to go for it?"

"No...I wish I could."

"Why not?" River asked.

"For one, I can't break the rules. I already did it once and look what happened..."

"Never forget that incident," he said with a laugh smile.

"Secondly, her brother told me he would kill me if I ever made a move toward her. He's really protective of her, not that I blame him. Men must throw themselves at her like crazy."

"You could take him," he said dismissively.

"But the biggest problem of all is the fact she thinks I'm gay."

"Why the hell does she think that?" He almost knocked his beer over as he reacted.

"Because I'm her brother's escort."

"Oh…" He nodded in understanding. "Everything is working against you, man."

"I know. I guess I could wait until my assignment is finished."

"You just want to fuck her, right?"

"Well, that's all I can think about when I'm around her. Shit, it's all I can think about when I'm *not* around her."

He rubbed his chin as he looked across the bar. "I'd go for it anyway. Hit on her, fuck her, and tell her to keep it to herself."

"But that's the problem," I said. "If I do go for her, she'll know her brother paid me to be his boyfriend. I'll blow his cover. I can't throw him under the bus like that. He's a good guy."

"Then find a beautiful girl to help you forget about her."

When I scanned the bar, all I saw was a bunch of trolls. "Now that I've seen the promise land I don't want anything else."

"The attraction will wear off," he said.

"Or grow more intense," I said bitterly.

"Let me see this girl," he said. "Introduce me."

I gave him a venomous glare. "Just because I can't fuck her doesn't mean you can."

"Hey, don't take everyone down with you," he said in mock offense.

I couldn't get this girl out of my mind. Why did the hottest chick in the world have to present herself now? When I couldn't have her? I'd give her my best moves and get her in the sack in less than an hour. But now I had to keep my hands to myself—literally.

***

Max texted me. *Want to come over?*

Your parents are going to be there? I was surprised they came around so fast. It'd only been a week.

No. I have to keep up pretenses for my sister.

I wanted to see Ophelia but I also didn't want to see her. Being around her was like being near a fire in the dead of winter. You wanted to get close because you needed that warmth, but when you got too close you got burned instead. *I'll be there soon.*

Cool.

When I arrived at his door, he answered it. "Hey." He pulled me inside and gave me a big hug.

I returned the embrace. "Hey." I didn't kiss him because it was against the rules. And I was glad Max obeyed it. No way in hell would I kiss a dude—for any amount of money.

"I missed you."

Since he was being affectionate, I knew Ophelia was nearby. That made my heart race. "I missed you too."

"You guys are so cute," Ophelia said from the couch. She was wearing yoga pants and a t-shirt. Her hair was in a bun but she looked amazing. Her face was free of make up but I preferred her that way. Her eyes sparkled like gems.

"Hey," I said as I approached the couch. "How are you?"

"Well," she said. "You?"

"Good." I stared at her and put my hands in my pockets. It was so hard for me to be platonic toward her. I wanted to sit beside her and give her my best moves. I could charm her and fuck her in no time.

But that wasn't a possibility.

"I got Battlefield," Max said. "You want to play?"

"Sure." Max was the straightest gay guy I knew. He acted just like one of my friends. He was cool, easy to get along with, and he liked beer, sports, and music.

Max set up the game and then we played. I kept glancing at Ophelia. She was reading a book and didn't pay attention to us. But I paid attention to her. Even when she wore yoga pants, her legs were irresistible. I wanted to rip them off and kiss the area, especially the area between her legs.

My thoughts became so distracting that I got killed—ten times in a row.

"Dude, where's your head at?"

Between your sister's legs. "Just haven't played in a long time…"

"Can I play?" Ophelia asked.

She played video games?

"No," Max said. "My boyfriend and I are playing."

"Well, your boyfriend sucks," she jabbed.

"You think you can do better, sweetheart?" I stopped playing and gave her my darkest smolder.

"I *know* I can do better," she challenged.

"Then get your ass over here and prove it."

"I will." She moved to the spot next to me then snatched the controller. "Watch."

I stared at her face and inhaled her scent. I was particularly close to her, close enough for a kiss if Max wasn't sitting there.

She got into the match then killed Max immediately.

With an astounded expression, I turned to her. "Damn…"

"Told you so." She stuck her tongue out at me playfully.

I wanted to grab it with my teeth then pull it into my mouth.

They kept playing, and Ophelia was demolishing him.

I decided to even the scales. Honestly, I didn't care about the game that much. Watching her have serious skill during a video game only heightened my attraction to her. But I wanted a reason to touch her. I stuck my fingers in the area between her ribs and tickled her.

She laughed as she tried to keep playing. "You're a terrible person."

I smiled then kept tickling her. I loved the feel of her waist. Her muscles tensed as I touched her, and I could feel the power underneath her clothes. She was slim and her ribcage was tiny. I could wrap my hands completely around her. "No. You're a terrible player."

She laughed in a high-pitched away, practically screaming. "Stop." Tears came out of her eyes. "You're going to tickle me to death." She fell off the couch and abandoned her controller, trying to protect her stomach.

I moved down to the floor with her and kept tickling her. "Gotcha." Being on top of her was making me hard. Her tits shook every time she moved, and a few strands of hair came loose from her bun. They framed her face and made her look like she just finished a night of good sex in my bed. I tried to keep my pelvis away from her so she wouldn't feel my hard-on through my jeans. That would be bad.

"Are you guys twelve?" Max demanded.

"She laughs like a twelve year old," I said.

The doorbell rang and I stopped tickling her.

"Expecting anyone?" Max asked as he stood up.

"No," she said as she tried to catch her breath. She looked up at me with her arms protecting her stomach. "You're nothing but a big bully."

Max's back was to us so I leaned over her and got closer than I normally would. "You haven't seen anything yet, sweetheart." My face was dangerously close to hers. I knew I was being reckless but I couldn't help it. I loved flirting with her.

"I can be a bully too."

"Oh yeah?" I challenged. "You look like a pushover to me."

She pushed me in the chest but I didn't budge. I was a solid slab of steel.

"Never felt anything so hard in your life, huh?"

Her eyes narrowed on my face. "You're cocky, aren't you?"

"But I have a reason to be cocky."

"I beg to differ."

Max interrupted our banter. "It's for you." The door was shut and he stood in front of it.

I quickly got off her and tried to act like I wasn't discreetly hitting on her.

"Me?" she asked. "Who is it?" She sat up and fixed her hair.

"Cameron." He crossed his arms over his chest.

Ophelia noticeably stiffened, and not in a good way.

Who was Cameron?

"Get rid of him." Her voice came out cold. "I don't want to see him."

"You got it." Max walked back outside.

Ophelia returned to the couch and grabbed the controller. "You want to play—without tickling me?"

She acted like there wasn't a guy outside her door trying to see her.

"Who's Cameron?" I asked.

"Some asshole," she said vaguely.

"You want me to take care of it?" I asked seriously. "Because I can make sure he doesn't bother you again."

"I'm sure Max can handle it." She started the game.

Knowing some guy was bothering her pissed me off. I wasn't sure why.

Max came back inside. "He refuses to leave until you talk to him."

"Then he can stand out there until I go to work tomorrow morning."

Damn right, he can.

"Do what you want, Ophelia," Max said. "But in my experience, people don't usually give up until they have a face-to-face conversation."

"We already had one of those," she said coldly.

"It's just some friendly advice."

I tossed my controller on the couch. "I'll take care of it."

Both Max and Ophelia stared at me.

I crossed the living room then walked outside. A guy my height was pacing in the hallway. His hands were in his pockets and he looked stressed, like something important was on the line. He was less muscular than I was, but he was a decent looking guy, no comparison to me, of course.

He turned to me when he noticed me. "Who are you—"

I punched him hard in the face, making him stagger back then crash against the opposite wall. He slid down to the floor then wiped his nose on his arm. When it was covered in blood he looked up at me in shock. "Leave. Her. Alone."

He wiped his nose on the other arm. "Who the fuck are you?"

Ophelia came behind me then gasped when she saw Cameron on the floor. "What's going on?"

"Now get your ass up and leave," I threatened. "Or I'll crack both of your cheekbones."

Cameron used the wall for support as he rose to his feet. "Ophelia, who the hell is this?"

I answered before she could speak. "Her boyfriend. Now go before I make you go."

His eyes widened while he looked Ophelia.

"I warned you." I grabbed him by the back of the neck and threw him down the hallway.

"Jett, stop!" Ophelia commanded me.

I didn't lay another hand on him. Instead, I watched him get to his feet and stumble all the way down the hallway and out of sight. Then I turned back to her. "I don't think he'll bother you anymore."

"You didn't need to do that," she said. "That was totally unnecessary."

"He crossed you," I said seriously. "And that's what people get for crossing my friends."

She stared at me in surprise. Her eyes were wide and she looked at me in a new way.

"Let me know if he bothers you again." After I displayed my strength and exerted myself as the alpha, I walked back inside her apartment. She didn't come inside for a moment.

Max looked at me with wide eyes. "What the fuck was that?" he said in a low voice.

"Teaching that asshole a lesson."

"You don't even know him."

"I don't need to know him. He hurt Ophelia—that's all that matters.

***

Max preferred it if I stayed the night to keep up pretenses. It was important to him for his sister to believe in our hoax. She would defend him to his parents more if she understood him better.

He had an air mattress on the floor so that's what I slept on while he took the bed. Thankfully, he didn't make me act like we were getting down and dirty. That would have made it difficult.

But I couldn't sleep. All I could think about was Ophelia. She was on the other side of the apartment sleeping in her bed. What did she usually sleep in? Just her panties? A t-shirt? My imagination ran wild with me while I thought about it.

Unable to sleep and unable to stop thinking about that beautiful creature, I left Max's bedroom and headed into the living room. If I watched TV I would probably become distracted enough to fall asleep.

But Ophelia was already there. "Can't sleep?" She wore a baggy t-shirt and shorts.

"No…guess not." I sat on the other couch and tried not to gawk at her.

"Me neither." She changed the channel and searched for something to watch. She finally settled on *The Matrix*. "Is this okay?"

"It's a great movie."

She pulled a blanket over herself and stared at the screen.

I stared at her.

When she turned her eyes on me, I quickly looked away. "You really didn't need to beat him like that."

"Actually, I did."

"You don't even know what he did to me. He could have forgotten to pay me back for something."

"Well, now he'll pay up."

She continued to stare at me.

"I don't know you that well, but I could tell his presence made you extremely uncomfortable. You don't strike me as the kind of person that easily gets mad. So, whatever he did, it was substantial. If he thinks he can hurt you and get away with it, he's wrong. He's got me and Max to deal with."

Whatever anger or resentment she had toward me disappeared. "I guess I have another brother now…"

"And friend."

She pulled her hair over one shoulder and faced the TV.

"What did he do, Ophelia?" I assumed he was an ex-boyfriend who blew his chance with her. *Idiot.*

"It's a long story…" She pulled the blanket closer to her, covering that beautiful body.

"Well, I can't sleep anyway. And if it's really boring, at least it'll put me to sleep." I gave her a smile so she knew I was kidding.

"Alright." She played with her hair while she spoke. "We started dating about two years ago but I would say the relationship ended about a year ago. He stopped being sweet to me. He didn't open doors for me anymore. He didn't ask me how my day was." Her voice dropped further, taking on a tone of sadness. She looked down at her hands while they played with her hair. "He stopped kissing me as often. Sex didn't seem all that fun to him anymore. My feelings hadn't changed so I wasn't sure why they had changed for him." She looked at the TV, not really watching it.

He stopped kissing her? Stopped wanting to have sex with her? It sounded like he was gay.

"I've been waiting for it to get better, assuming we've hit a rough patch or something, but it seems to be getting worse. Last week we were having lunch and he wouldn't stop checking out our waitress. He flirted with her, and when she wasn't around, he still searched for her. He wasn't at all interested in the fact I was there. He didn't care in the least. I used to be the only woman in the room. Now I'm just one of the many, and I'm the bottom on the list." She stopped playing with her hair and sighed. "So, I dumped him and stormed off."

"You should have dumped him," I said quickly. "And I should have punched him harder."

She rested her hands in her lap. "I know guys always check out other girls—"

"They don't," I interrupted her. "If you were my girlfriend, I would never look at another woman." I blurted that out without thinking. "If I ever wanted a girlfriend…if I wasn't gay."

"You're sweet," she whispered.

"I mean it. You deserve to be with someone who adores you, in the beginning and years down the road. This guy sounds like a douchebag."

"He is."

"And you shouldn't feel bad that I hit him."

A small smile stretched her lips. "My brother is protective but I've never seen him flip out like that…"

"Well, you can tell who calls the shots in the relationship."

"I'm glad my brother has someone who has a backbone. I know you'll look after him."

I want to look after you. "Yeah…"

She watched the movie for a while, and Keanu Reeves managed to escape the matrix.

I wanted to keep talking to her. I enjoyed it. "When did you start working in fashion?"

"As soon as I graduated college three years ago. I love my job. I know that may sound stupid, but I care about clothes, matching, and accessories."

"I don't think it's stupid," I blurted. "You want to know what I think is stupid?"

"What?" she asked.

"Doing something you don't love. Now, that's stupid."

She gave me that bright smile I dreamed about. She was so cute that I wanted to scream.

"And I love fashion." Not really. But I was gay, so I was supposed to, right?

"You do?" she asked.

"Yeah. I mean, look at me."

"I've only seen you in jeans and a t-shirt."

"We both know I rock it," I said with a cocky smile.

She laughed, and the sound was beautiful. "I won't deny that. You work out a lot?"

I didn't want to sound like an asshole with my response. "I try to go as often as I can."

"Then you must go everyday," she noted. "To look like that..."

"I do," I said. "Two hours a day." I knew that was excessive but it was part of my job. The rest of the guys were forced to do the same thing. No one would pay us to escort them if we weren't in tip-top shape.

She whistled. "That's dedication."

"I care about having a healthy lifestyle."

She released another laugh. "No, you care about getting laid."

I gave her a guilty smile. "You caught me."

"It's okay. It's why ninety-nine percent of people have a gym membership."

"You hit the gym," I said. "I can tell."

"You can?" she asked.

"Don't play dumb," I said. "A girl doesn't have a body like that unless she does dead lifts and free weights."

She turned her full gaze on me, and her emerald eyes reflected the light from the TV. "You can tell, huh?"

"I've looked at you." I stared her down with confidence. "You have toned thighs, rounded shoulders, and your ass is...nice." I had to be careful with my choice of words. I had to remember I was gay. But gay guys would say that, wouldn't they?

"Well, thank you," she said with blushed cheeks. "That means a lot coming from a gay man."

I shrugged. "I may like men but that doesn't mean I don't know what's attractive in a woman." And she was the definition of attractiveness. "What gym do you go to?"

"Crunch Fitness."

"On fifth?" I asked.

"Yeah."

"No way. I go there too."

"I've never seen you before," she said. "And I would have remembered you."

What did that mean? Was she attracted to me? I hoped so. I couldn't really tell with her. But I knew she liked me. She wouldn't be up at three in the morning having a conversation with me if she despised me. "I'm pretty unforgettable." I flashed her a wink.

She rolled her eyes. "I didn't realize Max liked cocky guys."

"Really? He loves *cocky* guys."

She laughed. "Don't be crude."

"And I've never seen you there. And I definitely would have remembered you." *Because I would have taken you on my sheets directly afterward.*

"Why would you have remembered me?" she asked. "Unlike you, I'm not memorable."

This girl had a weird self-image of herself. Did she not know how gorgeous she was? Did she not realize she made every guy around her hard all the time? Did she not realize she was the most beautiful woman I'd ever laid eyes on? "Now I'm hating your ex-boyfriend more. He should have made you realize just how damn unforgettable you are." I held her gaze long after I said it, wanting her to know how serious I was. "If you were my girl, you never would wonder if you were memorable."

She held my gaze before she looked away. "I'm sure you make Max feel that way…"

That's right, I'm gay. Ugh, I kept forgetting. "Yeah…"

She picked at her fingernails in her lap.

"You want to work out together?" I asked. "It'll be fun."

"Work out with me?" she asked incredulously. "I'm sure we have two very different work out regimes."

"And we can learn from each other. Besides, I want to get to know you better."

"Why?" she asked as she turned her gaze on me.

"You might be my sister-in-law someday. I want us to have a relationship." Not really. I wanted her to get close to me. When this assignment was finished, I'd go after her with everything I had. Hopefully, she wouldn't say no.

"I guess that's true," she said. "It would make Max happy."

"And I'm a great friend to have around. We can go shopping together too."

"Shopping, huh?" she asked.

"Come on, a gay man's opinion is priceless."

"Well, I have Max…"

I shook my head. "He doesn't know anything. Trust me."

She considered the offer for a moment. "Okay. Let's do it."

I felt my body flush in excitement. I would be spending time with Ophelia alone without her brother breathing down my neck. Maybe she would notice me the way I noticed her. I wasn't sure how I was going to make this work, but it was going to work somehow.

chapter 4

Ophelia

I walked into Crunch Fitness with my bag over my shoulder. I just got off work so I'd been sitting at my desk all day. Since I didn't move around much, mostly did typing and phone calls at my desk, I knew had to do some serious weight training. If not, those muscles would weaken. *Use it or lose it, right?*

I changed into my spandex shorts, Nike running shoes, and pink workout top before I walked onto the gym floor. I searched for Jett but saw a swarm of heads turn my way. I ignored them then kept walking.

"Hey, sweetheart." Jett came from my left and I almost fell over. Not because he scared me but because he didn't have a shirt on. His wide chest was chiseled and defined. It was hard like a slab of concrete. I remembered how it felt when I tried to push him away. His shoulders were rounded and muscular, but he wasn't overly bulky like some guys in the gym. He was ripped and toned. His chest led to the eight-pack chiseled down his stomach. The grooves were so hard it looked like an ice cube tray. He was already a little sweaty, and that just made the sight even more hypnotizing. I stared at him then looked at the V of his hips. The noticeable lines disappeared into his shorts, and a thin line of hair beneath his belly button went with it.

Oh my fucking god. He was hot.

"You okay there?" A smug look was on his face, like he knew exactly what I was thinking.

The arrogance in his voice brought me back to earth. "Yeah…just a little warm."

"I wonder why…" He didn't drop his smile.

"You're lucky you have something to be so cocky about."

"You think I'm hot, don't you?" He got into my face, his lips close to mine. He stared down at them like he wanted a taste. But then he directed his eyes back to mine.

"You're my brother's boyfriend. Of course I don't think you're hot."

"You're full of it. Just admit it." He pressed me further.

"I admit your body is…wow."

His eyes lightened in approval. "Why, thank you."

"You're welcome. But you forced the comment out of me."

"Or did I?" He stepped away and headed to a work out area near the mirrors. "Let's do squats." He grabbed a bar and put weights on the ends.

I grabbed my own but put far less weight on mine. I tried to be toned, not bulky.

"You can do more than that, sweetheart." He put an extra five pounds on each end.

"I don't think you know what I'm physically capable of."

"Yes, I do," he said. "I can see your ass."

"Now look who's checking out who," I argued.

"But that's the difference between you and me. You're attracted to men. I'm not attracted to women."

It was because of that reason I didn't take his comments seriously.

"Let me see what you can do." He faced me and crossed his arms over her his chest.

Seeing him shirtless was incredibly distracting. I'd seen attractive men before but Jett was different. His body looked like it belonged in a magazine. His hair was always messy but in a sexy way. And he was charming even when he was being cocky. I planted my legs apart then grabbed the bar on the floor.

Jett moved to my side and watched my form. "Nice…"

I did three sets of ten.

"You've got perfect posture. I'm impressed. And I told you that you could handle that extra weight."

"I'll feel it tomorrow…"

"I'll give you a nice massage." He winked at me then did his set. He had much more weight than I did, at least over a hundred pounds more. But he did it without looking like it was an exertion. He finished his set then placed the bar on the ground. "Now that's how it's done."

"Are you ever *not* cocky?"

He shrugged. "Not sure. Probably not." He smiled at the end so I knew he was joking.

"Have you ever done yoga?"

He turned to me with an incredulous look. "Me?"

"Whom else would I be talking to?"

"Sweetheart, real men don't do yoga."

I crossed my arms over my chest. "Have you ever tried it?"

"No. I'm too busy doing manly things."

"It's really hard…"

"Maybe for you."

"I think you should try it," I said as I put my hands on my hips. "I don't think you can handle it."

"Sitting on a mat and doing human origami? Yeah…I think I'll be finc."

"Fine, let's do it," I said. "I bet you won't survive."

"And what are we betting?" he asked.

"Twenty bucks?"

He shook his head. "I don't bet money with women. How about this? If I win, which I will, you have to have dinner with me. If you win, which you won't, you can pick something."

"Why would you want to take me out to dinner if you win?" I asked.

He shrugged. "It's what I want. And what do you want?"

I thought for a moment. "You have to hold all my bags while I go shopping."

"Deal." He extended his hand to shake mine.

I took it and gave him a firm shake.

"You've got a good grip, sweetheart. I bet you know how to grip other things with the same level of skill…"

I swatted his shoulder. "Don't be gross."

"Hey, it's true." He put his bar away and grabbed new weights. "How about shoulder presses?"

I let the comment go then racked my bar. "Okay."

We did a few other exercises together. Surprisingly, Jett was a good workout partner. He pushed me when I didn't feel like giving it my all, and he made the work out fun. When he wasn't being cocky or arrogant, he was pretty fun to be around.

By the end of the session, we were both hot and sweaty.

"Want to get shakes next door?" he asked.

"Sure." I usually just munched on a protein bar but it would be nice to have something different.

After we showered in the locker room, we headed next door and ordered our protein shakes. Then we sat at a table in the rear.

"So, tell me about you and Max," I said as I sipped my shake.

"What about us?" he asked as he leaned back and drank half of his in a single gulp.

"Like, how are you together? My whole life Max has been straight, and then a month ago, he tells me he's gay. I guess I have a hard time picturing it."

He took another sip of his drink before he spoke. "We're pretty much just friends who enjoy doing...other things together. We both like playing sports, playing video games, and our personalities are similar. There's really not much more to it."

"Are you romantic together?"

He looked down at the table. "Yeah, I guess. We kiss and stuff..."

He seemed uncomfortable talking about their relationship to me. Perhaps I was prying. "Sorry I asked. It's really none of my business."

"It's okay, I'm not offended. I just wasn't expecting you to ask."

"I really admire both of you for being honest about who you are." I really meant that. Our country had become more progressive but there was still prejudice going on. They would never be fully free, not in their lifetime.

"Thanks…I really admire Max. He's strong and doesn't let the negatives drag him down. He faces everything head on without blinking. He's a really cool guy. You're lucky to have him as your brother."

"I know I am."

"And your support means a lot to him—to both of us."

I rested my hand on his and felt the scorching heat. He looked down at our joined hands. "I'm just glad you guys are happy. That's what I want for my older brother. He deserves it." When I pulled my hand away, he still stared at the area where we once touched.

"Yeah…"

"So, how long have you been gay?"

"Uh…" He sipped his drink again. "Since I became an adult. I just came out to my parents and told them the truth. It's been fine ever since."

"And they support you?"

"Yeah, they don't care," he said quickly.

"That's nice. I hope my parents feel that way soon."

"Give it time," he said quietly. When he glanced around the Shake Shack he spotted a blonde at the counter. Like he was afraid, he turned to me and pivoted his body so his back was to her.

I thought his behavior was odd but I didn't ask him about it.

He kept his face averted and tried to pretend everything was normal—even though it clearly wasn't.

The blonde turned his way after she paid for her drink. Then her eyes narrowed in recognition.

"She's coming over here." I thought it was fair to give him a warning.

"Damn."

She reached him and tapped him on the shoulder. "Hi, Jett. Long time, no see."

He sighed then turned in his chair. "Hey, Lizzie." He didn't seem happy to see her.

She was very pretty. Even I was checking her out. She had bright blonde hair, crystal blue eyes, and a body most girls would kill for. "So, you didn't have time to call me back?" Attitude was in her voice.

"I guess I lost track of time," he said with a shrug.

What the hell was going on here?

She put one hand on her hip and glared at him with hatred. "So we have a wonderful time together—"

"Look." His voice grew serious, like he was about to command soldiers into battle. "I never said I was going to call you. It's your fault for making the assumption. I told you exactly what I wanted from the beginning. If you want to be treated differently, I suggest you behave differently."

For a moment, it looked like she was going to throw her shake all over him. But she took the high road instead and marched off.

When she was gone, Jett relaxed. "Sorry about that…"

"What was that about?"

"Sometimes when I meet girls..." He suddenly faltered and cleared his throat. "When I make friends with a girl, they understand that I'm gay. But then they...fall in love with me and hope that I might possibly be straight—for them. And when I'm not, they get really upset." He finished the rest of his shake.

I would have thought that was a weird explanation if I hadn't spent time with Jett first. He was very charming, charismatic, and of course, gorgeous. It wouldn't be difficult to fall for him, not with those blue eyes and messy brown hair. And he was fun to be around. My brother landed the jackpot. "That must be tough."

He shrugged. "It is what it is."

***

When I came home, Cameron was standing outside my door. I froze because I wasn't expecting him. After the way Jett sucker punched him, I hoped he would stay away.

I guess I was wrong.

His lip wasn't swollen anymore, and the bruise around his eye had disappeared. When he spotted me he straightened and faced me head on. "You have a boyfriend now?" His voice was cold.

That was the first thing out of his mouth? That was all he cared about? "Yeah. And he's just as good in bed as he is at punching people." I walked to my door even though he was right beside it.

"What the fuck, Ophelia? You get mad at me for checking out a waitress but you've had a boy toy on the side?"

I crossed the threshold then turned around, blocking the door. "I never had someone on the side. Is it really that hard to believe that another man would want to scoop me up?" Jett's words came back to me. "Because I'm memorable to someone even if it isn't you." I slammed the door and locked it.

Cameron banged on the door and called my name.

I ignored it. He would go away eventually.

Max came out of his bedroom. "You want me to take care of him? And not in the way Jett handled it?"

"No. He'll give up eventually." I tossed my gym bag and purse on the table.

Max eyed me in my spandex. "Good workout?"

"Yeah, actually."

He nodded. "So...I wanted to talk to you about something." He sat down at the kitchen table and proceeded to ignore Cameron as he banged on the door.

"What's up?" I grabbed a bottle of water then sat across from him. My muscles were sore from working out with Jett. With a body like that, he clearly knew his way around the weight room. I was a little embarrassed he caught me checking him out. But he was probably used to it even though he was gay.

"What do you think of Jett?"

That was an odd question. "I love him. Why?"

"He...doesn't make you uncomfortable?"

"No...why would he?" Was I missing something? He was funny and sweet. He was a bit cocky sometimes but he honestly had something to be cocky about. He was too handsome for his own good.

He shrugged. "Just curious."

"He and I worked out together today."

Both of his eyebrows shot up. "You did?" He didn't seem pleased.

"Yeah, he showed me a few different exercises and pushed me when I wanted to slack."

He nodded slowly. "And you enjoy spending time with him?"

"I told you, I love him. I think he's great, Max. Honestly, you landed the jackpot with him."

"You think?" he asked in surprise.

"You don't...?" *Was Max totally blind to his own man?*

"Of course I do," he said quickly. "But...he doesn't make *you* uncomfortable? You aren't lying to me?"

What on earth was he talking about? "Absolutely not."

"You're sure?"

"Yes, I'm sure. I like hanging out with him. He's my friend. Isn't that a good thing? I assumed you would want your sister to get along with your boyfriend."

"Of course I do. As long as he doesn't bother you."

"He doesn't bother me, Max."

Dangerous Stranger

"Okay." He finally backed off, and the sound of Cameron banging on the door continued. He glanced at the door then turned back to me. "Determined, isn't he?"

"It's the first time he's showed any determination for our relationship in a year," I said. "How flattering…"

"You doing okay?" he asked with a sympathetic look.

"I'll be fine," I said dismissively.

"I'm always here to talk. You know that."

"Yes, I know." I gave him a quick smile. My brother wasn't just my family but he was also my friend. When he said he needed a place to live, I didn't mind letting him live with me. In fact, I liked it. It was nice not to feel alone in my large apartment.

"Just making sure." He rapped his knuckles on the table before he headed back to his room.

***

When I got off work, I got a text message from Jett.

Sweetheart, how about that yoga?

I involuntarily smiled when I spotted his name on the screen. *You aren't going to survive.*

That's what you think. There's a class in fifteen minutes. You game?

For a gay guy, he talked like a straight guy. *I'm game.*

See you then, sweetheart.

Even when I put my phone away, I was still smiling. Perhaps Jett was making my breakup a lot easier. He gave me confidence when all I felt was doubt, and he reminded me I was worth something even if Cameron acted like I wasn't. He distracted me, spent time with me. And he made me smile while he did it.

After I changed into my yoga pants and sports bra, I grabbed a mat and walked inside the work out room. Jett was already there, in the back corner with a black yoga mat. He was shirtless like last time we worked out together. And of course it was distracting. *Extremely distracting.* I hadn't seen a guy this good-looking…ever. I was glad Cameron thought he was my boyfriend. I'm sure that stung.

Jett turned his gaze on me when he noticed me, and those blue eyes darkened a shade. His eyes quickly scanned my body, looking at my stomach and hips, before he turned back to my face. There was a dark smolder deep within, and his face was clean like he'd shaved that morning. I couldn't tell what I liked more; when he shaved or when he didn't. That's how beautiful he was. "I thought you were going to chicken out."

"Me?" I asked, distantly offended. "I don't back down from anything." I lay down the mat then sat on top of it and began to stretch.

Jett watched me with his full attention.

"You aren't going to stretch?" I asked as I moved.

"You stretch after a workout." His arrogance was right on the surface.

"Well, this is a different kind of workout." I pushed my feet together and made a diamond with my legs.

He turned to see a man leaning over his wife as he pressed her legs back, stretching her hamstrings and quads. Then he turned back to me. "How about I help you stretch instead?"

A shiver ran down my spine and I had no idea where it came from. I completely misinterpreted what he said and I had no idea why I did it. Jett was gay and spent the night with Max often. Why was I distantly hoping he was straight, seeing things that weren't really there? "I think I can handle it."

"I'm always here if you change your mind." He winked at me.

I lay on my back then lifted my hips into the air, stretching my quads.

Jett watched me, his eyes centered on my stomach. "You have a beautiful body." His voice carried his seriousness.

I relaxed and lay on the mat. "Are you checking me out?" One corner of my mouth curled into a smile.

"It's not rocket science to understand when someone is attractive." He looked away, staring at the wall.

"So, that was a yes."

"I appreciate art, and I think a fit body is art."

"Uh-huh…"

Now his lips curled into a smile. "Maybe I was checking you out. Maybe I wasn't."

"Well, I'm not your type. So you're wasting your time."

He turned back to me and his gaze bore into my skin. But he didn't speak.

The instructor emerged and started the class.

"Since I'm a nice person, I won't tease you," I said.

"Since I'm a gentleman, I'll still take you shopping even when I win."

"You're the cockiest man I've ever met." I sat up and crossed my legs.

"Well, look at me. I have something to be cocky about."

I smacked his arm playfully. "How does Max put up with you?"

"He looks at me. That's how."

I rolled my eyes dramatically.

He playfully pushed me over, making me roll onto the mat. "Keep it up and I'll tickle you next time."

The instructor began the class and we did light stretches. Jett didn't struggle with those. But I knew he would falter the more intense the workouts became. He was a muscular guy, and men tended to be less flexible than women.

When we moved into the crane, Jett struggled to remain upright. Eventually, he couldn't keep his balance and fell over.

A quiet laugh escaped my lips and I tried to hold it back.

He shot me a glare and tried again but he couldn't get it.

Then we moved onto another complex move where we had to touch our fingers to our toes. Jett could barely reach past his knees.

"I wonder what mall we should hit…"

"Brat," he whispered.

Jett couldn't even attempt the final move of the session and just watched me. My ass was in the air and I had the strangest feeling he was staring at it but I knew that couldn't be right. He was probably staring at the guy in the front row.

When we finished, we rolled up our mats then stacked them in the corner.

I gave him a smug look. "Not so cocky now, huh?"

He looked away as he walked beside me. "Yoga is lame anyway."

"For people who can't do it…"

He nudged me in the side playfully. "Did it ever occur to you that I might have let you win? Because I'm a nice guy."

"No," I blurted. "You just suck."

He nudged me again. "I'll tickle you if I have to."

"You wouldn't dare," I challenged. We were near the locker rooms and I was almost free.

Jett shoved me against the wall then pinned me down. Then he tickled me fiercely.

I started giggling. "Stop! We're in public."

His chest pressed against mine and he blocked me in. Mercilessly, he tickled me and made me laugh uncontrollably. "Watch your mouth next time." He tickled my stomach for a moment before he finally stopped. But he remained pressed against me with his face above mine.

I was suddenly aware of how close he was. His chest was sweaty and it was broad and strong. His breathing fell on me, and I suddenly thought of things I shouldn't. Never in my life had I been attracted to a gay man, but sparks were flying on my end. Perhaps my feelings were just misplaced because I hadn't received any attention or affection in a long time. I hoped that was the case. Jett was my brother's boyfriend. If I were truly attracted to him, that would make me a horrible person. I cleared my throat then walked around him. "I'm going to shower."

"I'll see you in a few."

When I got into the shower, I made sure it was on cold.

***

Jett wore basketball shorts and a t-shirt while he waited for me outside the gym.

I wore leggings and a loose top, wanting to be comfortable because I was exhausted. I'd probably take a long catnap the second I got home.

"So, when do you want to go shopping?" he asked in a disgruntled voice.

"Sore loser, huh?"

"I just let you win because you're pretty and you're my boyfriend's sister. So, don't get too arrogant."

"Like you?" I countered.

He glared at me with his eyes but his lips contained a smile. "Where do you want to go, sweetheart?"

"The mall, of course."

"And I'll carry your bags for you like an obedient dog."

"Great," I said excitedly. "And since I'm such a nice person I'll have dinner with you afterwards. It's a win-win."

His eyes lightened in excitement. "Yeah?"

"Yeah."

"Sweet." He nudged me in the side. "You're pretty cool, Ophelia. You must rub off on Max."

"He rubs off on me," I corrected. "He's my hero."

"He is a pretty cool guy," he agreed.

"Alright. How about tomorrow after work?"

"Sounds like a plan," he said. "You want to meet there?"

"Sure. Outside of Bloomingdale's."

"Okay."

I didn't want to go home because Cameron would probably be there. I released an involuntary sigh, which came out louder than I meant.

"Everything okay, sweetheart?" Concern was in his eyes.

"Yeah. I just don't want to go home."

"Why is that?"

"Cameron will probably be waiting outside my door like usual."

He quickly became rigid. "You can come to my place. You're always welcome."

"No, it's okay. I have to face the music sometime."

"Then I'll go with you." He started walking.

"Whoa, wait." I caught up to him. "You don't need to do that. I can fight my own battles."

"You don't have to." He walked forward with a determined expression on his face.

"Really, it's fine." I grabbed his forearm and felt the muscles and veins.

He let me touch him and didn't pull away. "I'm not going to let him harass you. I'll take care of it."

"Don't hit him," I said quickly. "Please."

"Why?" He looked me in the face. He deserves a lot worse for treating you like dirt.

"Violence doesn't solve anything. Don't lower yourself."

He sighed and kept walking. "Fine. But I'll still give him a piece of my mind."

At least he agreed not to hit him.

When we reached the hallway of my apartment, we saw Cameron standing outside the door. He looked up when he saw me, and he opened his mouth to speak but abruptly closed it when he spotted Jett.

Jett sauntered forward, his shoulders squared and his jaw tense. A maniacal gleam was in his eyes, and even I was a little scared of him. He came right up to Cameron and got in his face. "Leave my girl alone. Or I'll snap your neck." He continued to pressure Cameron until Cameron backed up into a wall. He held Jett's gaze for a moment before he looked away, finally acknowledging that Jett had more power. "Do you understand me?"

Cameron wasn't easily subdued. He was aggressive and territorial. The fact Jett could scare him and make him look like a total pussy was impressive.

"I didn't hear you." Jett didn't back off.

"I'll just go…" He stepped away.

Jett grabbed him and shoved him against the wall again. This time he pinned him down by the throat. "I didn't hear you."

Cameron grabbed the hand that covered his throat but didn't try to pull it off. "Okay…I understand."

"Do you really?" Jett asked with a dark voice. "Or am I going to see your sorry ass next time I take my girl home?"

"I'll leave her alone," he said quickly.

Jett finally backed off. "Now run."

Cameron walked away, gave me one final look, and then disappeared around the corner.

My eyes turned to Jett. "He's never scared of anything."

He was still in an angry mood. "Then he's never met me." He waited for me to get the door open.

After I snaked my keys out, I got the door open. I tossed my bag on the table and Jett followed me inside.

Max came out of his bedroom. "Good. No crazy ex-boyfriend to deal with today?"

Jett watched him but didn't react. He didn't even look happy to see him.

"Well, Jett scared him off," I said. "But he didn't hit him this time."

Max approached Jett then hugged him.

Jett flinched for a moment before he returned the embrace. "How are you?"

"Good. You?" Max pulled away then regarded him for a moment.

I watched them, noting their odd behavior. They didn't kiss each other like I would expect most couples to do. "Why don't you guys ever kiss?"

"Sorry?" Max asked.

"You guys never kiss," I said. "What's that about?"

Max cleared his throat and put his hands in his pockets. "We don't want to make people uncomfortable."

"Well, it doesn't make me uncomfortable," I said. "You guys can be yourselves around me." I opened the refrigerator and grabbed a bottle of water.

"Well, thanks…" Jett's voice trailed away.

I sat at the table and took a deep drink. "So…no word from Mom and Dad?"

"No." Max sighed then sat down.

Jett did the same, sitting beside him.

"You want me to talk to them?" I asked.

"Not sure…" He ran his fingers through his hair. "It's been weeks…I would think that would be enough time for them to accept it."

I shrugged. "I don't see what the big deal is. They need to get over it."

"Well, I'm their only son," Max said. "Perhaps that's why it's difficult to digest."

Jett patted him on the shoulder. "They'll come around. Just give it time."

"I hope so," Max said.

"They're going to that benefit next weekend," I said. "I'm assuming they want us there."

"Maybe just you this time," Max said.

"You're going," I said firmly. "Even if I have to take you as my date you're going."

Jett flashed a smile in my direction. I guess he wasn't upset over Cameron anymore.

Max turned to Jett. "Want to do something tonight?"

"Sure. What did you have in mind?"

"How about I stay at your place?"

"Sounds like a plan." But Jett didn't seem too excited about it.

I excused myself from the table. "I'm going to go in my room and read. I'll see you later."

"I'm going to leave so I'll see you sometime tomorrow," Max said.

"Okay, have a good time." I turned to Jett. "And thanks for having my back."

He gave me a serious look. "I always have your back—and your front."

***

Throughout work, I wondered how my shopping adventure with Jett would be. He didn't seem like someone particularly interested in fashion, but he claimed he was. And he was gay, so his sense of style was automatically better than mine.

He was on my mind a lot lately and I couldn't shake him. I remembered the way he scared Cameron off without any effort. He was cocky, dominant, and aggressive. He emitted so much testosterone he had enough for two full-grown men. Sometimes I couldn't believe he was gay.

My thoughts were shattered when there was a knock on my office door. I stopped thinking about Jett's physique, cocky smile, and smartass comments long enough to join reality. "Come in."

The door opened but someone I didn't expect walked inside.

Cameron.

I froze while I stared at him. Irritation and anger washed through me in waves. I was starting to boil but I had no outlet to let out the steam. It was one thing to harass me at home, but it was completely different to come to my work. I slowly rose to my feet and shot him a glare. "Close the door."

He did as I asked then approached my desk.

"How dare you come to my office." I kept my voice low. Yelling would draw attention. "I have an image to protect. This is totally unprofessional."

"You didn't leave me any choice," he said coldly. "This is the only place I can find you without your boy toy."

"There's nothing to say." I gave him my best look of menace. "We're done. Move on. You didn't love me anyway. So what's this really about? Wounded pride? You want to dump me instead? Would that make you go away?"

He rested one hand on my desk and stared at it. Then he looked up at me. "I've been doing a lot of thinking over the past few weeks…"

"I didn't realize you could think at all."

He ignored the jab. "You were right about everything. I didn't treat you right and you deserve a lot more. Somewhere down the road…the relationship just got old. But that wasn't your fault. It was mine."

I didn't expect him to say any of this. Cameron never apologized for anything. I figured he would argue with me until he got his way.

"I should have worked harder to keep this relationship alive. Seeing the way I hurt you and the way you walked away…made me realize the mistake I made. I know it doesn't seem like it but I really do love you. And I want to prove that." He looked me in the eye.

I crossed my arms over my chest.

"And the fact you're already with someone else…makes me realize what I lost." He swallowed the lump in his throat. "I really want another chance. I'll be better this time."

"He's not my boyfriend."

His eyebrows shot up. "Then what is he? Just a hookup…?" His voice faltered at the end.

"No. He's my brother's boyfriend."

He flinched at my words. "Max? He's gay?"

"He just came out a few weeks ago. He's been dating Jett for a while. We've become good friends and he was just trying to protect me from you."

"That guy is gay?" he asked incredulously. "He just doesn't seem…"

"I know." I couldn't agree more. "But he is."

He nodded slowly. "You have no idea how relieved that makes me feel." He turned back to me, apology in his eyes. "Baby, I love you. Please give me another chance. Remember the way we used to be? How amazing it was?"

How could I forget?

"Let's try to get it back. Please."

I'd never heard him say please so many times.

"You really hurt me…" *More than I would care to admit.*

"I know…I'll make it up to you."

Could I really let it go? I would always remember the way he was so much more interested in the waitress than he was with me. But he didn't cheat on me. We'd grown distant with each other but we never betrayed each other. And our relationship used to be magical. I wished it had stayed that way. "I can't just jump into a relationship with you again. As petty as it sounds, I don't trust you."

"Okay...can we start dating again? Take it slow?" There was desperation in his eyes. "I'll do anything to keep you, baby. Whatever you want."

His determination was what I wanted—months ago. But I couldn't deny his charm. Maybe our old relationship was too far gone to get back but I wanted to try. Maybe I was chasing something that would always be out of my reach but if we could make it work...I wanted it to work. "Okay."

A smile stretched his lips. "Okay? You'll give me another chance?"

"I'll date you again," I said. "But that's all I can give you. If you prove your sincerity then...we'll go from there."

He released a deep sigh, and joy lit up his face. "Thank you so much. You won't regret it."

"I hope not, Cameron." *I really hope not.*

Chapter 5

Jett

"So, you want to see my place?" I asked as Max and I walked up the sidewalk.

"Actually, no. I was just using that as an excuse."

"An excuse for what?" *What would he be doing that he didn't want his sister to know about?*

"To see my boyfriend." He kept his hands in his pockets as he walked.

"Whoa, what?" I stopped in my tracks. "You have a boyfriend?"

"Don't tell me you're jealous." A joking smile was on his lips.

This was a crucial piece of information. If Max already had a boyfriend, he wouldn't need my services anymore. Then I could go for his sister. I was tired of pretending to be gay around her. My attraction to her was only increasing. Instead of just wanting her on my sheets, I was thinking of her in other ways. I wanted to spend time with her, take her out to dinner, and lay in the park with her. But I couldn't make that happen if I had to pretend I wasn't deeply attracted to her. "If you have a boyfriend then you don't need me anymore." I wanted to skip then click my heels together.

"No, not at all," he said. "I've had a boyfriend this whole time."

Now I was even more confused. "Then what do you need me for?"

"I told you. You're the ideal man. My parents are more likely to accept me if I bring home a man they like."

"And why wouldn't they like the man you're actually seeing?" *Was he ashamed of him?*

He rubbed the back of his neck. "I have a very specific taste in men. And I don't think my parents would like it…"

"Is he a horse?" I blurted.

"No." He chuckled lightly.

"Well, I'm sure your sister wouldn't care. You can tell her the truth."

"No. She's a terrible liar. I love her to death but she can't act the part if her life depended on it."

I was starting to feel hopeless. "So, are you expecting me to do this forever? That's not fair to your boyfriend."

"No, of course not. You're just doing the dirty work so he doesn't have to deal with it. It's the best thing for us."

I didn't care about doing the heavy lifting. I just wish Ophelia could know the truth while I did it. Spending time with her was only making me obsessed. Her ass looked like a nectarine in those spandex shorts, and I wanted to run kisses up and down her tight stomach. Whenever she laughed, I melted. Whenever I touched her I didn't want to stop.

"Just stay the course. It won't last forever."

A minute without Ophelia felt like forever.

Max came closer to me and lowered his voice so no one could hear, not that there was anyone to eavesdrop. "My sister thinks you're just her gay friend. She doesn't think there's any attraction to her on your part. I don't care if you want to continue to spend time with her—as long as she's okay with it. But if you bother her or make her uncomfortable, I will break every limb you have." There was seriousness in his eyes. "I mean it. If you really want to go for her after this assignment is over, I won't stop you. But I can guarantee she'll reject you."

"Why?"

"Because you're already in the friend zone. And once you're there, you can't get out."

I disagreed with that. I felt a connection between us. I even felt heat between us. Whenever she looked at me, especially when I was shirtless, I caught a glimpse of desire. There was sparks between us even if I couldn't see them. Maybe she didn't realize it because she thought I was gay, but there was something there. I just had to spend more time with her so she wouldn't date someone else. Then once I was free of my contract, I would tell her exactly how I felt. And I would tell her my dick only wanted her pussy.

"Just be careful." He gave me one final look before he walked up the sidewalk.

I stood there and wondered what kind of man Max was hiding. Was he hideous? Was he disfigured? I guess I would know eventually.

***

I stood in front of Bloomindale's and waited for Ophelia to arrive. I wondered what she would be wearing. Shorts? A dress? I hoped she wouldn't wear pants. I wanted to see those beautiful legs. Imagining them wrapped around my waist was my greatest fantasy.

But I had to act like I cared about fashion. How would I pull that off? I always wore jeans and a t-shirt, and I went shopping maybe once a year. It wasn't a hobby of mine.

Max said Ophelia really believed I was gay, so every time I flirted with her, discreetly hit on her, called her sweetheart, and every time I tickled her she thought it was just a friendly gesture on my part.

Did that mean I could get away with more?

Just when I started to think about it, she appeared. "Hey yoga master."

I looked up and saw her in a yellow sundress. It reached passed her thighs and she wore nude pumps. A teal cardigan was over her shoulders and her purse hung at her side. Her hair was curly and long.

My god, she looked beautiful.

I stood up, and without thinking, I embraced her. I'd never hugged her before and I wasn't surprised by how much I loved it. My chin rested on her head and I pulled her chest against mine. I could feel her tits covered in the padding of her bra and I loved the sensation. She was tiny in my arms and I wanted to hold her forever. Her scent came into my nose and I inhaled it deeply, enjoying it. I wondered if she enjoyed me as much as I enjoyed her. "You look beautiful." I reluctantly pulled away so she wouldn't feel the hard-on in my jeans.

"Thank you." She looked up into my face and her eyes danced with the green color. They reminded me of freshly mowed grass in the summer. I could even smell it just by looking at her. "You look nice too."

"Nice?" I asked in disapproval. I was only wearing dark jeans that hung low on my hips and a shirt that highlighted my powerful chest, but still. I tried on several different outfits until I found something that would soak her panties. "Come on, sweetheart. I look better than *nice*."

"You get cockier every time I see you."

"Just admit it." I pressed my face closer to her and I resisted the temptation to kiss her. "I look hot."

She rolled her eyes.

"We aren't shopping until you give me a better compliment."

She sighed but I could tell she was amused. "You look too handsome for your own good."

"That's better," I said. "Thank you."

"You're welcome," she said with a light laugh.

I automatically wrapped my arm around her waist as we walked inside. I realized my mistake then pulled it away and acted like I did nothing wrong. It was just an impulse I couldn't control. I could cross the line a little bit but I still had to pretend I preferred men. But after meeting Ophelia I couldn't believe any man would be gay. How could they not be attracted to something so beautiful? "Where to first, sweetheart?"

"I need to find a new dress for the benefit."

"I can help with that." I walked beside her and kept my hands to myself.

"You do a lot of dress shopping?" she teased.

"I like to experiment." I smiled in her direction.

She laughed. "You don't strike me as the drag type."

"I'm adventurous."

"And my brother certainly doesn't strike me as that type."

"You don't know him the way I do."

She chuckled.

We entered the dress shop. It was a swanky place. I could tell by the way the employees were dressed and the music on overhead. Plus, the prices were ridiculous.

Ophelia moved through the aisles and studied each gown. "Hmm…"

I scanned the dresses on display then found a black on with lacy sleeves. But it was also backless. I loved backless dresses. Nothing was hotter than woman's slightly sculpted bare skin. And I would love to see Ophelia's. I snatched it then picked the smallest size I could find before I came behind her.

"I like the pink one."

"Wear this." I handed it to her.

She examined it, feeling the sleeves and noting the lack of material in the rear. "It's cute…and a little scandalous."

"I think it would look amazing on you. Try it on."

She debated it for a moment before she agreed. "Okay. But let me look around more."

"No, I think this is the dress." She would look damn fine in it, and with a pair of heels she would look stunning. I'd have a hard time not blatantly hitting on her and dragging her into the bathroom so I could kiss her everywhere. "Let's hit the changing room." I grabbed her by the wrist and guided her to the fitting area.

She reached a door then walked inside.

I sat on a chair and waited for her to present it to me when she was finished.

She opened the door again. "What are you doing?"

What did she mean? "Sorry?"

"Get in here."

My heart raced in my chest and steam came out of my ears. She wanted me to go in there…and watch her change? That sounded fucking awesome but I also felt guilty. If she knew I was straight she never would invite me. "It's okay…I'll wait out here."

"Don't be stupid. Get in here."

I knew I should be a gentleman and refuse her advance. But I wasn't a gentleman and never had been. Trying to pretend I wasn't extremely excited and about to explode, I walked inside and joined her. "Are we allowed to do this?"

"I change in front of my girlfriends all the time. I hate walking out there when a bunch of strangers are walking by. It's awkward."

And this isn't? I sat down and tried not to stare at her.

She turned her back to me then took off her cardigan. After she hung that up, she unzipped her dress and peeled it away.

Holy shit…

She stood in her cheeky panties then grabbed the black dress off the rack.

I shoved my fist into my mouth because I wanted to scream. Her ass was gorgeous. It was perky and round, and her toned thighs looked delicious. My hard cock was about to snap through my zipper.

Fuck…fuck…fuck.

She pulled the dress on and covered herself.

"Oh, thank god."

"Sorry?" She looked at me over her shoulder.

"Uh...thought I saw a spider." I glanced at the corner.

"Oh." She turned back around and adjusted her dress. Then she stood in front of the mirror.

I already saw her fine ass and that was a glorious sight. But seeing her in the skintight dress that highlighted the curve of her back and the prominence of her tits was just as lovely. Her slim waist made an hourglass figure and the sleeves of her dress added a classy touch.

"You were right," she said. "It's a perfect fit."

I probably knew her body better than she did. "It's what I'm here for." I'd never been so horny in my life. I wanted to bend her over and fuck her right then and there. I shouldn't have come in here. Now that sight of her gorgeous behind would be burned into my mind every time I jerked off and thought about her.

She turned around and peeled the dress off.

No...not again. Don't look. Don't do it.

She pulled it off then grabbed her original sundress.

I looked. And while I was ashamed of myself for having no strength to resist, I enjoyed it so much that I didn't care. I wanted to pull her panties off and bite each cheek. I wanted to stick my face between her legs and smell her scent.

Thankfully, she got her original dress on and pulled the cardigan over it.

But it was too late. I would have a hard-on for the rest of the day—rest of the year, actually.

"That's the quickest I've ever found a dress," she said. "I'm taking you with me every time."

I'll have to think of an excuse next time. "I'm a man of many talents." Resisting temptation wasn't one of them.

We left the changing room and she purchased the dress. Then she handed me the shopping bag. "We had a deal, right?"

I was going to offer to carry it anyway. "Yep." I took it from her hand and carried it as we walked out.

"Are there any stores you want to go to?" she asked.

"No, not really."

"Dinner?"

"Sure. I'm starving."

We walked down the sidewalk until we agreed on a French bistro. When we walked up to the door, I opened it for her.

She slightly reacted, like she was surprised I had manners. Then she walked inside. She did the same thing when I pulled out the chair for her before I sat across from her.

Did none of her boyfriends treat her like a lady? It baffled me when gorgeous women were with assholes. They deserved so much more and they didn't even realize it. I really didn't want Ophelia to be one of those girls. She deserved the best. I wasn't the best, especially after that fiasco in the changing room, but I would try to be the best if she gave me a chance.

We ordered then sipped our wine while we looked at each other.

"I hope Max isn't mad I'm hogging you."

He couldn't care less. "We spent plenty of time together when he came over the other night."

"Where is your apartment anyway?" she asked.

"Right by Central Park."

"Wow. It must be really nice then."

I didn't like to brag about my wealth. And I hated to listen to other people do it. "I like it," I said with a shrug.

She smiled at me, like she knew I was trying to be humble. "You're the perfect man, Jett."

I almost knocked over my wine. *What did she say?* "Sorry?"

"You're the perfect guy," she repeated. "You're smart, sweet, and polite. You're playful and not stiff all the time. And you're gorgeous. My brother hit the jackpot with you. It doesn't surprise me that he's gay. I might even judge him if he weren't."

What did that mean? She thought I was the perfect guy? Did that mean she thought I was perfect? If she knew I was straight, would she want me? I tried to think of a response but nothing came to mind. So I reverted back to being an arrogant asshole, what I do best. "Tell me something I don't know."

She narrowed her eyes on me, and she didn't seem to buy what I was selling. "You're full of it. I know you are.

You're a really humble guy but you try to hide it with this cocky attitude."

"Maybe...maybe not."

She sipped her wine again and dropped the subject.

Could I really keep doing this for much longer? As lame as it sounded, I was falling for her. When I first met her she was just a hot piece of ass I wanted to sink my teeth into but now I wanted so much more. I wanted to open every door for her, take her shopping on my dime, and walk her home. I was turning into a pussy-whipped douche.

But I didn't care.

"Do you want to have kids?" she asked.

It was a random question and shattered my previous thoughts. "Yeah. Do you?"

"I want two. A boy and a girl."

"Same here." *Not really.* I hadn't thought much about it. Before she came along I couldn't even picture myself getting married. But if I was spending all this time with her and not getting laid, then she was damn special.

"How would you guys do that?" she asked.

What was she talking about? "Do what?"

"Have kids. Adoption?"

I kept forgetting I was gay. "Yeah, that's the best option. So many kids in the world don't have parents as it is. We could give them a home."

She smiled and her eyes softened. "That's sweet. I would love to be an aunt to your kids."

I forced a smile but it was so fake.

"Do you think you guys will get married?"

God, no. How did I handle this? Max had a boyfriend so our relationship would end eventually. I didn't want to say I was making a lifelong commitment if I knew it would end, and probably soon. "Not sure. It's too soon to tell."

She nodded. "I guess I understand that. Have you had a serious relationship before?"

I didn't know how to handle her curiosity. "A few years ago…it didn't work out." I kept my answers vague. That was probably the smart thing to do.

"I'm sorry," she said.

"It's okay. Max is better anyway." He and I would probably be good friends if we weren't in such an odd situation. "How about you?" I asked. "Anyone serious before Cameron?" Honestly, I didn't want to hear about her former lovers. The idea of anyone touching her but me set me off. I practically ripped off Cameron's head last week. I'd never been so territorial before. I was claiming her as mine even though she didn't belong to me. But I felt rude if I didn't ask her the same questions in return.

"Not really," she said. "I dated a few guys here and there but no one really caught my attention. Then I met Cameron and all of that changed." She released a heavy sigh as she thought of distant memories.

"You'll find someone better. Just give it time." *Me. You'll find me. And I'll make you so damn happy.*

"Well..." She touched her wine glass but didn't take a drink.

Well what? What did that mean? "Yeah?"

"Cameron came to my office a few days ago."

My heart fell into my stomach and I felt deathly ill. My entire body tensed like I was about to get into a major car accident. I was on defense, waiting for an attack I knew would be fatal. I didn't want to hear her following words but I couldn't not hear them. "And?"

"He apologized for everything and he said he was wrong. He never apologizes for anything..."

Please tell me this is a joke.

"He said he wanted another chance. I told him I couldn't jump into a relationship again but I agreed to date him and see where it goes." She stared at her wine glass as she spoke, not looking at me.

I felt like my entire world crashed. "Why would you agree to that?" My voice came out far more hostile than I meant.

She flinched because she was so surprised.

"This guy treated you like shit. He doesn't deserve a second chance." I stared her down and knew I was giving her a threatening look even though I wish I wouldn't. I was just too pissed off.

"But what we had before—"

"Is gone. You can't get it back. And it's clear he didn't want to get it back until you walked away from him. Don't do this, Ophelia."

She remained calm. "I know you hate him but—"

"I'm going to share a secret with you. And it's going to hurt."

She closed her mouth and just listened.

"If a guy isn't interested in having sex, it's because he's getting sex somewhere else. Whether he's in love with you or not, you're hot and he'll fuck you because it's convenient. The only reason why he would stop is because he found someone better to fuck."

She didn't flinch as she listened to me.

"I'm not saying this to hurt you, but I can promise you that's what happened. When you walked away, he realized what he was missing. You suddenly became more desirable. But it doesn't change what he did."

"Cameron isn't the cheating type."

"And what is the cheating type?" I demanded. "Cheaters are liars and they are good at covering their tracks. If he didn't want you to know about it, he would have covered it up and buried it."

"You're making assumptions when you don't even know him."

I was growing irritated with her. She was too damn smart and beautiful for this bullshit. "If he blatantly gawks at another woman when you're right in front of him, he doesn't respect you. And if he doesn't respect you then, what makes you think he'll respect you when you aren't around? I'm telling you, Ophelia. I've had a lot of dog friends. I know how they are."

Dangerous Stranger

"I still think you're being presumptuous."

I leaned back in my chair and tried not to scream. "You broke up with him for a reason. Don't crawl back to him just because you're scared."

She suddenly became defensive. "I'm not scared. Cameron is the only guy I've ever really cared about and—"

"He didn't care about you," I snapped. "What makes you think he won't act like this again? There's nothing to prove that he won't."

"And there's nothing to prove that he will."

My blood pounded hard in my ears. I wanted to flip the table over.

She took a few seconds to calm down. "Jett, why are you so upset about this?"

Because you should be with me. "Because you're my friend. And I protect my friends."

"And I really appreciate that." She rested her hand on top of mine. "But I'm a big girl and I can take care of myself."

I want to take care of you.

"Let it go."

I knew pressing this argument wouldn't change anything. She obviously already made up her mind and she wouldn't change it back. She was blind to the womanizer she was seeing. "Okay. I'm sorry." I leaned back in my chair and pretended to be calm. Her hand left mine and I suddenly felt cold.

She gave me a smile but it was forced. "Are you going to the benefit with Max?"

"If he attends at all," I said quietly.

"I'm sure he will. He belongs there just as much as anyone else."

The conversation was still awkward and I had a feeling it would be awkward for a long time. Did that mean she would take Cameron? I'd have a hard time not shoving my fist down his throat, grabbing his heart, and yanking it out and watching him die right in the middle of the dance floor.

Ophelia caught my look. "Everything okay?"

I gave her the fakest smile I could muster. "Yeah. Just fine."

***

Max took a bite of his sandwich then looked out the window.

I ordered food but I didn't eat it because I wasn't hungry. "Did you know your sister got back together with that asshole Cameron?"

He chewed for a long time before he swallowed. "She mentioned it."

"Then you need to tell her to dump him. Forbid her from seeing him."

Max was about to take another bite but stopped when he heard what I said. "Do you know Ophelia...? I have better odds of telling a hippo what to do than boss her around."

"What happened to being protective of her?" I demanded.

"Ophelia is a grown woman who can make her own decisions. Secondly, what do I need to protect her from? He doesn't treat her right and I agree with that. But he doesn't hurt her."

"But he cheats on her."

That caught his attention. "Why do you say that? Have you seen him?"

"No…"

He cocked an eyebrow. "Do you have any evidence of this treason?"

"Well, no…"

"Then I'm not intervening. I already told Ophelia Cameron isn't right for her. If she wants to date him anyway despite what I said, repeating those words won't change her mind."

I wanted to smash my fist through the table.

"Jett." His voice came out quiet. "I get that you want to be with my sister but breaking them up isn't the answer."

"I'm not doing this because I want her," I snapped. I ran my fingers through my hair in agitation. "I'm doing this because I know he doesn't deserve her. He's a jackass who doesn't treat her right. I care about her, and I'm not going to let her settle. If she picked a good guy who adored her I'd let it go."

"Would you really?" Disbelief was in his voice.

"Yes." I looked him in the eye as I said it. "And I know she's not in love with him. It's as obvious as the change of the seasons. You can't necessarily see it when it happens, but you know it's occurring."

Max finished his sandwich then wiped his mouth with a napkin. "If Ophelia told me not to be with my boyfriend just because she had a hunch that he was a bad guy, do you think I would listen to her?"

I already knew the answer so I didn't say anything.

"Me speaking to her is pointless. The only way you can really get rid of him is prove your suspicions. And I don't see how that's possible."

A light bulb went off in my head but I didn't share my idea with Max.

"Honestly, you know what I think you should do?" Max asked.

"Hmm?" I wasn't sure if I wanted to know.

"Forget about my sister." He said it harshly and without sympathy. "It's not going to happen, and even if she is single by the time our assignment is over, you really think she's going to want to be with you?"

"Why is that so hard to believe?" I snapped. "I'm a great guy. I treat her right, make her feel good about herself, and I tell her she's the most gorgeous damn thing on the planet. She and I have a great time together, and I can tell she really cares about me. She may be out of my league but that doesn't mean I don't have a shot."

He didn't argue with any of that. "That's not what I meant."

"Then spit it out."

"When she finds out you're straight and this was all a ploy, how do you think she'll feel? Happy? Or tricked?"

I hadn't thought about it that way.

"The odds are slim to none." He threw his trash away and headed for the door. "I suggest you find someone else to fuck so you can get over her."

***

I told the guys the whole story at the bar. "And she just went back to him. I couldn't believe it." I was still fuming about it.

River rubbed his chin before he lowered his hand. "Seriously, how hot is this girl? Because you're acting like a circus clown right now."

I ignored the comment. "I know he has skeletons in his closet. There's no way a guy would treat her like that unless he had a thing on the side or he was gay. I need to uncover it so I can expose him. Then she'll ditch him."

Rhett rubbed his forehead. "You know how crazy you sound right now?"

I kept going. "I need you guys to tail him day and night. You can take shifts. We're going to find whatever he's hiding. We're going to get it on video and we're going to bring this fucker down."

"You think we don't have lives?" Troy asked. "Because I have shit to do."

"I'll pay you," I blurted. "Just do this for me."

"You don't have to pay us," Cato said. "We got your back."

Troy sighed like he wished Cato hadn't said that.

"Around the clock?" River asked in surprise. "What about between one and five a.m.? You really think something is going to go down then?"

"Probably not," I agreed. "But I want someone on him all hours of the day."

"What about you?" Rhett asked. "Are you participating in this?"

"I wish," I said. "He'll recognize me and know I'm up to something. I can't do it."

"How convenient," Troy said sarcastically.

"So, you guys are with me?" I asked to clarify.

River shook his head. "This chick better be as hot as you claim."

"She is," I said. "But that isn't the only reason why I'm doing this."

"Then why are you doing it?" Rhett questioned. Judging the slight smirk on his lips, he already had a suspicion.

I didn't see the point in hiding it. "I really care about her."

"Wrong answer," River said. "You're pussy-whipped."

"How can I be pussy-whipped if I've never had her pussy?" I demanded.

"Exactly," Troy said.

I cocked an eyebrow because I missed the point everyone else got.

***

Max invited me over, and I hoped Ophelia would be there. She and I hadn't spoken much since she told me she and Cameron were back together. It was hard to look at her and not scream.

How did a perfect woman like that not realize how damn perfect she was?

I entered the apartment and embraced Max like I usually did. Touching and handholding was the only affection I would give, and fortunately, that was the only affection Max wanted anyway.

"How's it going?" he asked.

"Good." I discreetly scanned the apartment and looked for Ophelia. I didn't see her but her bedroom door was shut. "You?"

"Good. Nothing new. So, you want to play a game?"

"Sure." Maybe a game would distract me. I wondered what she was doing behind the door. Taking a nap? I'd love to sleep with her. Or maybe she was getting ready to go out. I didn't know but my curiosity wouldn't stop trying to figure it out.

"Cameron is picking her up and they're going out to dinner." Max answered the question I never asked. Maybe we were spending too much time together.

"Fuck," I said under my breath.

"Your life will be much easier if you just accept it."

"I'll never accept it." I played the game but wasn't really into it.

"Good luck with that."

Ophelia opened her door then stepped out wearing a purple strapless dress. Her eyes were highlighted with eye shadow and she looked like a wet dream. "Hey, Jett." She gave me a big and wide smile when she saw me. I'd seen her give countless fakes smiles to spot the real ones. Her eyes glowed like stars. She never had that look on her face when she spoke of Cameron.

"Hey," I said weakly.

"What do you think?" She twirled in a circle and posed for me. "You're the fashion genius."

She looked like a vision. "You look..." There was no word to describe exactly how she looked. Most gorgeous woman in the world would probably be over-the-top no matter how true it was. "Perfect."

"Great," she said. "Perfect from a gay guy is saying something."

I wish I were the man she was getting dressed up for.

"And my opinion is irrelevant?" Max asked.

She waved off his comment. "You would tell me I was beautiful even if I wasn't because I'm your sister."

Max laughed. "Whatever you say, sis."

The knock on the door announced Cameron's arrival. Ophelia grabbed her clutch and walked to the door.

I quickly turned to Max. "Help me."

"How the hell am I supposed to do that?"

"Let's make it a double date," I said. "Ask her."

He looked uncomfortable. "Dude, you need—"

"Please." I wasn't above begging.

He sighed at the desperate look on my face. "Fine."

"Thank you. Thank you."

He stood up and came to Ophelia's side before she opened the door. "Hey, why don't we make it a double date?" he asked. "That would be fun, right?" It was obvious he was forcing it and had no real interest in going.

"A double date?" she asked.

"Yeah, we're both seeing someone at the same time."

"Uh…" She seemed hesitant at first. "Yeah, sure."

Phew. I was going to cock-block the shit out of Cameron.

"Cool," Max said.

Ophelia opened the door to Cameron. "Hey…" There was a slight hesitance to her movements.

"Hey." He leaned in and kissed her on the cheek. In his hands were flowers.

I tried not to roll my eyes. Guys only bought flowers when they did something wrong. And Cameron looked guilty.

"They are beautiful." She smelled them and placed them in a vase. "Thank you."

Cameron stepped inside. "You're welcome." Then he spotted me on the couch. He glared at me openly.

I glared back.

Ophelia caught the look. "I want my two best men to get along...okay?"

Cameron was silent.

So was I.

"You guys need to shake hands and move on," she said.

No fucking way.

Cameron looked like he felt the same way.

Max tried to clear the tension. "Well, we should get going. I'm starving."

"Whoa, wait." Cameron turned to Ophelia. "What does he mean by that?"

"Actually, we're going on a double date." Judging the cringe on her face she knew Cameron wouldn't be thrilled with the news.

He stepped toward her and lowered his voice. "I was hoping it would just be us...so we can talk about our relationship."

Think again, jackass.

"Well, I already said yes," she whispered.

He sighed in irritation but didn't press his argument. "Okay."

"Sorry," she said. "We'll have time later. Promise."

Good luck keeping that promise.

"Well, let's go," Max said.

I walked to the door and didn't hide the look of loathing on my face.

Cameron hated me just as much.

This should be a fun night.

***

We sat at the table and held our menus. I sat directly across from Ophelia, which I was grateful for. I'd rather look at her beautiful face instead of stare at that jackass.

Max sat beside me then rested his hand on my thigh.

I was glad he was taking charge of the affection we were supposed to share because I kept forgetting to. All I cared about was keeping Ophelia away from the pig that didn't deserve her.

I pulled out my phone and discreetly texted Rhett, who was on duty. *I'm at dinner with him now. Break into his apartment and search it.*

You want me to break the law?

You got my back or what?

There was a long pause. *How am I even supposed to get in there?*

Ask Cato for help. He can break into any door.

Fine. Tell me when he's on his way back.

K.

I put my phone back in my pocket then looked up to see Ophelia watching me with her hypnotic green eyes.

"Everything all right?" she asked.

It was about to be. "Yeah. Some friends wanted to go out tonight but I told them I was busy with my boyfriend." I gave Max a significant look.

He smiled back but the look didn't reach his eyes.

Cameron stared at me like I was a bug that just crawled over the table.

I decided to piss him off. "Ophelia, you look beautiful tonight. The dress really brings out your eyes."

"Oh, thanks." She blushed slightly.

Cameron narrowed his eyes at me.

"What are you getting?" I asked.

"Crème of asparagus soup and a side salad."

I was hoping she would order something better, like a steak.

"What about you?" she asked.

"Chicken with greens sounds good," I said. "So, are we hitting the gym together tomorrow?"

I wanted it to be clear I would be in her life whether Cameron was or not.

"Sure," she said. "It's nice to have a workout buddy."

Cameron just stared at me.

When the waiter came over, he took our orders. Max went first then Cameron. When my turn came, I ordered for both Ophelia and myself.

Judging the scowl on Cameron's face, he didn't appreciate what I did.

Well, you should have let her order first, asshole.

Ophelia sensed the tension. "Cameron is a lawyer," she said. "He's been practicing law for about two years."

"Nice," I said with a faked enthusiasm. "But that make sense. He's a crook and a liar for a living as well as in his personal life."

Cameron turned red in the face.

Ophelia looked uncomfortable.

Max tried not to laugh.

When the wine was brought, I uncorked it then poured Ophelia a glass.

"Thank you," she said quietly.

I poured mine and Max's, but left Cameron's untouched.

When he grabbed the bottle, I kicked him hard in the knee under the table and spilled the wine all over himself.

"Fuck," he said as he tried to move out of the way.

I sat still and looked innocent.

He tried to dab the wine out of his shirt with a cloth napkin but it wasn't helping. Then he turned on me with angry eyes. "You fucking asshole!" The whole restaurant turned in our direction at the commotion.

"He didn't do anything," Ophelia said. "Don't blame him."

This was too much fun.

He came around the table like he wanted to have a go.

I stood up and smiled, loving the opportunity. "I'd love to kick your ass, any place and any time."

He stopped his approach and glared at me in silence. Then he headed to the bathroom to wash up.

Ophelia cleaned up the remaining liquid on the table and dabbed at his seat. I helped her until everything was cleaned and contained. I was pretty sure Max knew what really happened and I was grateful he kept my secret.

"You guys didn't get any on you, right?" she asked.

"We're good," I said.

She returned to her seat and released a sigh. "Wow...this is going terrible."

"He's got slippery fingers," I said. "But he's stupid for trying to blame it on me."

"I'm so sorry," she said. "I thought he would be mature about this."

I tried not to smile. "It's quite alright."

A minute later, Cameron returned to the table. He sat down and his eyes were directed right at me. "You know what I think? I think you're straight and you're just pretending to date her brother so you can get to her."

Okay, he wasn't as dumb as I thought. "You're really onto something," I said sarcastically.

"Don't be ridiculous," Ophelia snapped. "Stop attacking Jett and let it go."

"Attacking him?" Cameron asked incredulously. "He was the one who kicked me in the kneecap so I would spill the wine."

"Yeah…you got me." I shrugged.

Ophelia rolled her eyes, clearly embarrassed and annoyed.

"This is the guy you really want?" I asked seriously. "Because he's not very bright, he's a liar, and he's a bit dense."

Cameron gripped the steak knife on the table.

Ophelia caught the movement and gripped him by the forearm. "Knock it off. Now."

Max just watched us silently, drinking his wine while trying not to laugh.

"Are you into five year old boys?" I asked. "Because that's what you're getting."

He looked like he might seriously stab me in the eye with his knife.

Now Ophelia held up her hand to me. "Knock it off. Both of you. You're both being childish and immature."

I zipped up my lips and took a sip of wine.

She turned her gaze on him and waved her finger in his face.

He drank his water since that was all that was left.

The food arrived and that gave us something to do. Cameron was already in the hole and I made their first date a total fiasco. Now Cameron looked like an insensitive jerk and I looked like the poor victim in all of this.

My plan was working too well.

We made small talk and Cameron didn't participate in the conversation. From what I gleamed from Max, he quit his job at the bank to be a writer, and Ophelia was supporting him so he could make that dream happen. It only made me more obsessed with her. She was selfless and kind. She had a generosity that I didn't see very often.

When the tab came, I snatched it and slipped my card inside. "Dinner is on me."

Ophelia gave me a bright smile. "That's so sweet, Jett. But you don't have to do that."

Cameron's eyes flared in irritation when he saw the affection his girl gave me. "No, I'll pay for it." He tossed my card at me then stuck his inside.

"Well, that was rude," I said. "I was trying to do something nice and you just swoop in and copy me?"

Ophelia gave him a look of disapproval.

Man, this was too easy.

"How about we split it?" he asked, trying to play nice even though it was causing his body to shake.

"I guess." I handed my card back.

After the bill was settled, we left the restaurant and walked outside.

"Let's go to my place," Cameron said immediately.

I couldn't let that happen, and not just because the guys were snooping around. "We should play Wii sports. That's so much fun." I nudged Max in the side.

"Yeah," he agreed but without much enthusiasm.

"Oh, I love Wii sports," Ophelia said.

Could she get any better?

"Let's play," she said to Cameron.

Cameron looked like he wanted to scream. "Whatever you want."

Sabotaging their date was a walk through the park.

***

"Hey, sweetheart. You want to be on my team?" I nudged her in the side as I sat beside her on the couch.

"Okay," she said. "But I think it's unfair to the other two."

"We'll be just fine," Max said in mock offense.

We played a few rounds and Ophelia and I won each time.

"You know, I think we're meant for each other." I was half joking, half being serious.

She laughed. "Maybe we are."

I got another glare from Cameron for that one.

When it was past midnight and everyone was tired, I kept making us play. I wanted Ophelia to be so exhausted that she wouldn't ask Cameron to spend the night. I couldn't sleep in Max's room and listen to them go at it. My ears would bleed.

At one in the morning, they finally called it quits. Ophelia could barely keep her eyes open.

I think I'm in the clear.

She finally stood up then adjusted her hair. "Well, tonight was fun."

Too much fun.

"I'll walk you out," she said to Cameron.

Take that, asshole.

A look of disappointment came over his face, and it was wonderful to see.

Together, they walked to the door then shared a few quiet words. Their night ended with a hug, no kiss. And then he left.

I tried not to smile. I took out my phone and sent the text to Rhett. *He's coming back.*

Thanks.

I put my phone away.

Ophelia stretched her arms over her head and yawned. "I'm hitting the sack. Good night."

"Night," Max said.

"Good night, sweetheart."

She leaned down and kissed Max on the cheek.

Then she came my way.

Was she going to kiss me? Was I going to feel those full lips on my skin? Would I really have a piece of her, no matter how small it was?

She leaned down then wrapped her arms around my neck.

I was nervous because I knew she was going to kiss me. I was so excited that I turned my head at the wrong time and got her lips on my mouth instead of my cheek. It was an accident but it was a good one.

Her lips touched mine then flinched when she realized where she landed. I moved my lips slowly, telling her it was okay. Then she kissed me back. The embrace lasted for two seconds at the most, but it was the hottest two seconds of my life.

She pulled away and looked at me with embarrassed eyes. She clearly didn't mean to kiss me on the lips.

"It's okay," I whispered. "I would never turn down a kiss from an angel."

The shame left her face, and a beautiful smile broke out instead.

I loved it when she looked at me like that.

"Good night, Jett."

My arms were still around her. "Good night. Now go before I tickle you."

"You always tickle me."

Because it's an excuse to touch you. "My hands have a mind of their own." *And so does my dick.*

She rose to her feet then walked into her bedroom.

Once the door was closed, I felt my lips with my fingertips.

I just kissed her. And damn, it was spectacular.

***

"Did you find anything?" I asked when I walked into Rhett's apartment. Cato was there and he sat at the kitchen table with lidded eyes like he was exhausted.

Rhett stood with his arms across his chest. "Nothing concrete. We found a few motel receipts, restaurant receipts, and this…" He pulled an orange bra and tossed it at me.

I cringed then dropped it, unsure whom it belonged to. "Where did you find it?"

"On the floor next to his bed," Rhett explained.

That could lead somewhere. "Is his apartment messy?"

"No, it's totally clean," Cato said. "Actually, the place is sterile."

I sat down and brainstormed. "Then this bra can't be Ophelia's."

"Why do you say that?" Rhett asked as he sat across from me.

"They've been broken up for almost a month. If she left it there before…I doubt he would leave it there the whole time, if he's so anal with having a clean apartment."

Cato nodded his understanding. "Good catch."

"It still doesn't prove anything," Rhett said.

"I think it does. He has a slut on the side," I said. "At least we know that."

"Actually, that's still an assumption," Rhett said.

"I know," I said as I snapped my fingers. "I'll take it to Ophelia's and ask Max to act like he found it in the wash. He'll ask if it's hers, and if she says no, then we know for certain he had some slut over."

"But we still can't prove anything," Cato said. "You need something better."

"I know, asshole," I snapped. "When we know there's someone else, we'll keep tailing him until he leads us to her. Then we'll get him good."

Rhett nodded. "Sounds like a plan."

"An excellent plan."

***

I got to the gym first like usual then spotted Ophelia walking past the windows in her work clothes with her gym bag over her shoulder. I was sitting on a bench and I immediately took off my shirt. I didn't normally workout shirtless but I had to catch her eye—and keep it.

After she changed in the locker room, she came out in spandex shorts and Nike running shoes that were bright yellow and blue. Her pink workout top was tight and she had a black sports bra underneath. Her hair was pulled back in a high ponytail and she looked sexy as hell.

I'd give anything to feel her legs wrapped around my waist.

"Hey." She gave me a smile but it didn't reach her eyes. She seemed different today, like something was on her mind.

"What is it, sweetheart?" I leaned closer to her, almost like I might kiss her. My hand moved around her waist like it belonged there. Her waist was so petite I could wrap my entire arm around her.

"Nothing." She pulled away and averted her gaze.

I pulled her flush against my body, which was a bad idea since I was starting to get hard. "Tell me. I'm not letting go until you answer." *And I wouldn't mind it if she didn't answer—ever.*

She took a deep breath before she spoke. And she didn't pull away. "I guess I'm really embarrassed."

"About what?" My face was pressed close to hers. I desperately wanted to kiss her again. It was so hard not to.

"I didn't mean to kiss you." Her cheeks flushed with color. "It was an accident and it was dark…"

I released a light chuckle. "It's not a big deal. It didn't bother me."

"I just don't want to make you uncomfortable."

"You didn't," I said firmly. "It's water under the bridge, honestly." My hand moved up her back to the area between her shoulder blades. *And it's not like I didn't kiss her first.*

"Okay…I'm glad we're good."

"We're amazing, baby." I walked to the bench press. "Okay. You're working your chest today."

She eyed the bench. "I've never done this before."

"I'll teach you and spot you. Come on."

She lay down underneath the bar.

I took off all the weight to see how she could handle the bar alone. "Try this. If it's too heavy I'll catch it."

"Okay." Without much effort she lifted the bar then did one rep. Then she returned the bar to the air.

"Good." I guided it back to the rack. "But that was too light for you."

"Don't put on too much weight," she said. "I don't have much strength in my upper arms."

"I beg to differ." I put ten pounds on each side. "This should be enough."

"You're spotting me, right?" There was a slight tone of fear in her voice.

"Sweetheart, I would never let anything hurt you." I said it with complete seriousness. I would protect her from everything. "But you can do this."

"Okay." She gripped the bar then slowly lifted it. Her arms shook slightly from the weight.

"You can do it." My hands remained on the bar just in case.

She did one rep then returned it to the air. "That's all I can do."

"You can do five. Come on."

"You're the worst personal trainer on the planet," she said through gritted teeth.

"Baby, I believe in you. Come on."

She did another one, sweat breaking out on her forehead. Then she completed the set and gasped for air.

I guided the bar to the rack and eliminated the weight off her frame. "I told you that you could handle it."

"My arms feel like Jello."

"But you're strong." I gripped one shoulder. "You're a tough girl. I like tough girls."

She continued to breathe until she caught her breath. "Are we done now?"

I chuckled. "Not even close."

She and I did a few other weight machines then jogged on the treadmill.

"Shouldn't we run before weights?" she asked.

"No, you burn more calories afterward because your body is tired." I ran beside her and felt a blonde checking me out. She was cute but she had nothing on Ophelia. She outshined everyone in the room.

After our cardio workout ended, Ophelia rested her hands on her hips. "Okay, I'm done for the day."

I smiled. "Are you sure you don't want to do some free weights?"

She nudged me in the side before she walked off.

After we showered and changed in the locker room, we met in the lobby.

"I'm going to be so sore tomorrow." She rubbed her arms like she was trying to get the kinks out.

"But it'll be a good sore." I opened the door for her before we walked outside.

"Well, I guess I'll see you next time." There was sadness in her eyes, like she didn't want to leave me.

I didn't want to leave her either. Maybe it was just a fantasy in my mind but I was starting to think she had feelings for me. That seemed so impossible but that didn't stop me from hoping. "Come over for dinner." I wasn't thinking when I blurted that out. I just didn't want to say goodbye to her.

"What's on the menu?" she asked, clearly intrigued.

"Tri-tip, potatoes, and greens."

"Yum, I'm not saying no to that."

"Then let's hit the road."

We walked side-by-side as we headed to my apartment.

"Should we invite Max?" she asked.

Oh yeah. He was my boyfriend. "I'll text him." I sent him a message. *If Ophelia asks, I invited you to dinner with us at our place but you said no.*

He responded back immediately. *No good can come from this.*

I'm doing it anyway. "He can't make it."

"Oh." She sighed. "He's been pretty busy with work."

"Yeah."

***

Ophelia looked around my apartment in awe. "Wow, you have a nice place."

"Thanks." I was glad she was impressed with me.

"Your pharmaceutical inventions must be really lucrative."

I had a really vague explanation of what my job was, and it was so complex no one really understood it. All that it really said was I was loaded. "I don't have any complaints."

"Can I have a tour?"

"Sure." Thankfully my maid just cleaned the place. I showed her the different bedrooms and bathrooms, and then I showed her my bedroom last. As soon as we were inside I felt a shiver move down my spine. I jerked off thinking about her on that bed too many times to count.

"How do you ever leave this place?"

"Only when really good company is involved." I gave her a smile then headed back to the kitchen.

She stopped on the way and looked at the pictures on the coffee table. "Who are these guys in the Mets jerseys?"

"My friends," I said. "I've known them forever."

"Wow…you guys are all…really good-looking."

"We both know I make the rest of them look like shit."

She chuckled. "You're right." She came into the kitchen and watched me open everything. "Can I help?"

"Yeah, cook this," I said. "I have no idea how."

She laughed. "How about I help you instead?"

"That's a fair compromise."

Together, we cooked. She took care of the potatoes and the veggies, and I cooked the meat. The savory smell of the food filled the kitchen, and my appetite increased by tenfold.

"Geez, I'm starving."

"Good thing the meat is done." I turned off the stove then walked into the dining room to set the table. She left her purse on the counter, and just when I was about to move it, her phone vibrated. I could see the screen clearly and Cameron was calling her. A moment of uncertainty passed through me. I wanted to delete the call so she wouldn't know she even got it but I thought that would violate her privacy. Instead, I shoved her purse into the closet so she wouldn't hear it vibrate if he called again. It was still wrong, but at least it was less wrong.

We sat down together and began to eat.

She ate quicker than I did, clearly famished after our intense workout.

"Want to know something interesting?" I asked.

"What?"

"Couples who work out together are more likely to stay together."

"Then it looks like we'll be friends for a long time." She kept eating.

I didn't like that she called me her friend but what else was she supposed to call me?

"Can I ask you something personal?

"You can ask me anything, sweetheart."

She sipped her water then looked down at her plate. "Have you ever been with a woman?"

I wasn't expecting that question. If I answered it honestly, I would have to say I'd been with over a hundred women. But that wouldn't make any sense. "No."

"No?" she asked. "Never?"

Why was she so interested? "I guess I haven't experimented much."

"Then how do you know you're gay?"

"How do you know you're straight?" I countered. "Have you ever been with a woman?" Just the idea got me excited.

"I see your point." She continued to eat.

"How many guys have you been with?" I assumed it was okay to ask since she'd asked me something personal.

She shrugged. "One."

"One?" I almost spit out my food. How was that possible? She was the most desirable woman on the planet.

"Yeah." She stopped eating and started to pick at her food.

"That's just...low."

"Yeah...Cameron is the only guy I've been with."

Now her behavior made a little more sense. "That's why you're trying to make it work with him."

Her eyes moved to mine. "It's not because I want my number to always be one. I've never cared about that. But...he was my first for a reason. If we have a chance to capture what we had we should try."

"In my experience, when the magic dies it's for a reason."

"I guess..."

"Do you love him?" I blurted.

She suddenly became uncomfortable. "What?"

"Do you love him?" I repeated.

Ophelia was clearly flustered. "Love is...difficult to explain."

Dangerous Stranger

"It's okay if you don't," I said. "I can tell you don't anyway." And I'm relieved.

"Well, I did at one point. But now…it's not there. We can get it back if we tried but—"

"Why are you forcing it?"

"I'm not forcing it—"

"There are so many other guys out there," I argued. "You could have whoever you wanted—literally."

She sipped her water again but I knew it wasn't because she was thirsty.

"Cut him loose and look for someone better."

"I…I don't want to talk about this anymore."

I sighed in irritation. Just when I got some progress with her, we retracted our steps. "I don't mean to come off too forward. I just really care about you and I want the best for you."

"I know, Jett."

"And…he was a total douche at dinner. He doesn't even have a personality. When I cornered him in the hallway, he backed off like a total sissy. That's the man you want?"

"I can't say I blame him for being intimidated by you. Look at you."

I leaned over the table and came closer to her. "The man you're with should intimidate anyone who crosses you. He should be strong, powerful, and protective." I'm all of those things. "If you were mine, I'd break any guy's neck just for looking at you. I'd make you feel like the sexiest woman in the world—all the time. And I'd make you come until you grew so sore you asked me to stop."

She dropped her fork and stared at me with wide eyes.

Okay...I probably took it too far.

Ophelia stared at me like she wanted to say something but couldn't find the right words.

I tried to shrug it off. "You know...hypothetically." She might realize I'm not just joking around. She might realize I wanted to fuck her on my sheets, right now, if she would have me.

"Cameron said something the other night..."

Oh shit. I knew where this was going.

"He thinks you aren't gay at all...but you're straight."

Fuck. Fuck. Fuck. How did I handle this?

She stared at me like she expected an answer. "You just don't seem gay," she said. "You're so...aggressive and flirty and...I don't know."

"Well, I am. Just because I don't fit the stereotype doesn't mean I don't fit under the label."

That seemed to convince her. "You're right. I shouldn't have said that."

"It's okay," I said immediately.

She picked at her food.

"Just because I'm gay doesn't mean I don't know how to treat a lady. And it doesn't mean I don't know just how beautiful, amazing, and valuable you are. Maybe you forget sometimes but I never do."

***

We watched TV on my couch, and I sat directly beside her.

"These leather couches are nice," she said.

I reclined them back with a click of a button.

"Whoa...snazzy."

We lay almost flat while we watched the screen. I had the urge to pull her into my arms and hold her. How would she feel lying next to me? I'd already felt her chest once against mine. But I wanted to feel more.

"I could sleep here." She rested one arm over the back of the couch. It deepened the curve of her back and I had to control myself from not devouring her. I wanted to press her into the leather as I thrust inside.

Damn, I'd never been this attracted to another person before.

"You know what would feel more comfortable?" I pulled her into my side and let her rest her head on my hard stomach.

"Concrete?" she asked with a laugh.

My ego increased at her words.

She looked up and smiled. "It's getting late. I should probably go."

I didn't want her to leave. I wasn't sure what I thought might happen, but I thought if we spent enough time together she would want to be with me. It was stupid and crazy but a guy could dream, right? "Yeah, probably."

She sat up then gracefully moved her fingers through her hair. Everything she did was sexy without even trying. I found myself staring at her more than I should. Sometimes it was out of my control.

She stood up then searched for her purse. "Hmm…I thought I put it here."

"Oh, sorry. I moved it for dinner." I opened the closet then lifted it from the hook. "There you go. I wasn't trying to rob you."

She chuckled. "If you can afford a place like this you don't need to rob anyone." Then she opened her purse and started to look through it.

I didn't want her to notice her phone, not until she was home and less likely to go out again. "Let me walk you home."

She stopped looking at her phone and turned to me. "It's okay, Jett. I can manage."

"I insist." I opened the front door and stepped out. "Max would never forgive me if I let something terrible happen to his little sister."

She stopped protesting. "Well, it'll be nice to have some company."

"There's the spirit."

She and I walked together down the sidewalk then toward her apartment a few blocks from my home. I wanted to walk her home anyway. The idea of her being out by herself at night made me uncomfortable. It was clear she could take care of herself but that didn't give me any assurances.

We reached her apartment and she snaked her keys out of her purse. "Thanks for walking me."

"Of course. Do you mind if I come in and say hello to Max?" I didn't care about seeing him. I wanted to spend as much time with her as possible.

"Sure." She got the door unlocked then placed her things on the entry table. "Max, your betrothed is here."

Max came out of his bedroom then embraced me like always, with little affection and no genuine interest. "It's always nice to see you."

"Yeah. Your sister and I were hanging out so I thought I'd walk her home."

"Thanks," he said. "She usually gets lost."

Ophelia sighed then rolled her eyes.

I leaned toward Max's ear. "The bra…" That was my cue to do what we already talked about.

He sighed like he thought this idea was stupid. "Fine. But you're crazy." He pulled away then headed to the laundry room.

"Are you spinning the night?" she asked.

"No. I've got a lot of things to do in the morning."

She nodded. "Well, I'm going to hit the sack. I'll see you later."

"Good night, sweetheart." I used to use the name on any girl I hit on. But now when I used it on Ophelia, it had a very different meaning.

Max came out of the laundry room holding a bright orange push-up bra. "Hey, Ophelia. Is this yours?"

She tilted her head to the side and examined. "Uh…no."

"Are you sure?" he said as he continued to hold it. "Because it's obviously not mine."

I watched Ophelia's face carefully.

"Believe me, I would know if I had a slutty bra like that," she said.

"Why is it slutty?" Max asked.

"It's so bright there's nothing you could wear over it," she argued. "Only a slut would have something like that."

So, it definitely wasn't hers.

"I don't know where that came from but it's not mine." She walked into her bedroom and shut the door.

When she was gone, Max tossed the bra at me. "So, what does this mean?"

"It belongs to some other bimbo." I shoved it into my pocket and felt gross for touching it. "Which means Cameron is cheating on her. Or at least he was."

Max crossed his arms over his chest. "That doesn't necessarily prove that…"

"What else would explain it?" I snapped. "This guy's apartment is sterile. He wouldn't leave some slut's bra on the floor forever. It's got to be someone recent—really recent."

"You were in his apartment?" he asked with a raised eyebrow.

"I wasn't. My friends were."

"Oh…that's much better."

"For being her brother, you don't seem that concerned about her boyfriend being a cheater," I snapped.

"Because you aren't giving me enough evidence to prove it," he snapped back. "If you did, like a picture or a text conversation I'd be the first one at his door to knock his teeth in. Until then, I'm not jumping to any conclusions."

"Well, I'll get you the proof you need."

He shook his head slightly. "You're obsessed."

"Yeah, I know." I turned to the door to walk out.

"Hold on," he said as he followed me.

"What?" I hissed.

"The benefit is this weekend. Can you come as my date?"

"I'm like your genie. I'll do anything you ask."

"My parents haven't actually invited me but I'm going anyway. The quicker you charm them and get them to accept me, the sooner you can tell Ophelia that you're psychotically in love with her."

"I'm not in love with her," I said darkly.

He clapped my shoulder and laughed. "Good one."

***

"So, what did she say?" Rhett asked when I slid into the booth.

"It's not hers." It was a victory but an empty one. I wish I were wrong about Cameron. I knew when Ophelia knew the truth she would be heartbroken. I'd rather spare her from pain even if it ruined my chances of being with her.

"Seriously?" Cato asked.

"There's absolutely no chance it's hers," I said. "She made it pretty clear."

"Damn," Rhett said. "So he is fooling around on her."

"And we have to catch him doing it."

***

I arrived at Max's doorstep wearing a three-piece black suit.

He whistled. "You look spiffy."

"Why, thank you." I stepped inside and looked at him. "You don't look too bad yourself."

"Whatever," he said. "We both know I look great."

And I wondered how great Ophelia would look.

"She's getting ready in her room." This guy could read my mind.

I couldn't wait to see her in that dress. It'd be hard not to rip it off of her. "How does she look?"

He shrugged. "I don't know. Like a troll."

I went into the kitchen then got four wineglasses. Then I poured champagne into each one.

"What are you doing?" he asked.

"Making sure Cameron doesn't last through the night."

He cocked an eyebrow while he watched me.

I poured the laxative powder into his drink then stirred it until all the powder was gone.

"Please tell me that isn't poison."

"It's a laxative—a powerful one."

He chuckled. "Poor guy."

"When I catch him in the act with his hussy you won't pity him."

"I hope for my sister's sake you're wrong."

"I'm not, unfortunately." I handed him a glass. "Hold onto this and don't put it down."

"Gotcha."

I held mine so it wouldn't be grabbed by mistake.

Ophelia came out of the room, looking like a godly queen. Her hair was pulled back, and a white gold necklace hung from her throat. The dress was tight on her curves, highlighting her hips and chest. I'd already seen her in the dress but I forgot how beautiful she looked in it.

She spotted me then kissed me on the cheek.

Goosebumps...

"You look handsome, Jett." She pressed her hand against my chest and felt my tie.

"And you look gorgeous, sweetheart." I wrapped one arm around her waist and rested my hand on her bare back. Her skin was smooth and warm. I wanted to touch it forever. Then I hugged her longer than what was socially acceptable.

She didn't seem to mind. "Champagne?"

I grabbed the glass that wasn't spiked. "Here you are."

She grabbed it and took a sip. "Good, you poured Cameron's for him. Now he won't knock it over." She chuckled at her own joke.

I released a fake laugh even though I didn't find it funny at all.

Then a knock sounded on the door.

"That must be Cameron." Ophelia left me then opened the door for him. "Hey."

He leaned in and gave her quick kiss.

I wanted to vomit.

"You look nice," he said.

That's it? Nice? Fucking asshole.

"You too," she said.

I hated this guy even more.

He came further into the room and shot me threatening looks.

This guy was the biggest pussy I knew so his looks meant nothing to me. I walked to Max then tapped my glass against his. "Let's do a toast." It was a stupid thing to do but I had to get Cameron to drink his glass, even just a sip.

"Good idea." Ophelia handed Cameron's glass to him.

This was too easy.

I held up my glass. "To a night full of fun, laughter, and joy." It was cheesy but whatever.

We clanked our glasses together then took a drink.

To my immense joy, Cameron took a long drought like he was thirsty.

I hoped that tux wasn't a rental.

"Let's head out," Max said.

***

I had a nice car so I insisted on driving it. Ophelia didn't seem particularly interested in wealth or money but I knew it would intimidate Cameron. So we piled into my brand new black Mercedes.

"This is a sweet ride." Max grabbed my hand and held it while I drove.

"Yeah, I like it." I kept my comments short.

"How much was this thing?" Max asked. "If you don't mind me asking?"

"One fifty."

He whistled. "Wow…"

Max asked me other questions about the car and I answered them all. Max was helping me and he didn't even realize it.

I glanced in the rearview mirror, not to check on traffic, but to check on Ophelia. To my misfortune, they were holding hands.

At least they wouldn't be for long.

Once we arrived at the country club at the outskirts of the city, Cameron farted—loudly.

Everyone heard it but no one laughed. I tried not to smile. And soon, the smell filled the car.

This is priceless.

Cameron looked out the window, embarrassed. Then he touched his stomach when it made a loud rumble.

"You okay...?" Ophelia kept her voice low.

"Yeah," he said. "I just...have an upset stomach."

Max shot me a look that said, "You're going to hell."

Silently, I said, "I know. But I don't care."

The valet took our car then we walked inside. Max and I didn't touch each other. I let him decide how he wanted to handle this. Ophelia hooked her arm through Cameron's, but it was clear he was experiencing more stomach pain judging the cringe on his face.

"You better hope he's cheating on her," Max said when we were out of earshot.

"He is. There isn't a doubt in my mind."

"You're going to feel like shit if you're wrong."

"I really doubt it," I said honestly. I grabbed two glasses from a passing waiter then handed one to Max. "So, what's the plan?"

"My parents are here and they don't know I'm coming. We'll feel them out and see how they react."

"I seriously hope they get off their high horse and stop being annoying."

"That makes two of us," he said as he took a drink.

I looked past Max's shoulder and watched Ophelia and Cameron talk quietly in the corner. His hand was on his stomach and they seemed to be having a deep conversation.

"I think Cameron is about to leave."

Max watched them. "Looks like your plan worked."

"Let's go over there."

We approached them and I pretended to be a caring guy. "Everything alright?"

"Cameron isn't feeling well," Ophelia said with concern.

"Oh no," I said, faking empathy. "I can give you a ride back."

"No, it's fine." He tried to act like there wasn't a small explosion going on down below.

"It's really not a big deal." I knew he would never take my offer.

"How about we call a cab?" Max asked.

"Yeah," Ophelia said. "Then we can head home."

We? No, that wasn't part of my plan.

"No, you stay here," Cameron said. "I can manage on my own."

"Are you sure?" Guilt was on her face.

"Really," he said firmly.

Max did a few things on his phone. "The cab is coming."

"I'll wait outside for it," Cameron said.

"I'll come with you."

"No, stay." He snapped at her and was being extremely rude. She was just trying to help. When people were in pain, it didn't bring out the best in them. But Cameron was being a huge ass.

Which worked in my favor.

Cameron left Ophelia standing there and walked outside.

"I hope he feels better," I lied.

Max rolled his eyes.

"Me too," she said quietly.

I came to her side and swooped in. "Cheer up. He'll be okay." I nudged her in the side and tried to get her to smile.

"You think?"

"I know." I put my arm around her shoulder. "Let's go get a drink."

"Yeah…okay."

Max cleared his throat and gave me a pointed look.

Oh yeah, I was supposed to be his boyfriend. "All three of us."

We walked to the bar and grabbed our glasses.

Ophelia's mind seemed elsewhere.

My finger moved down her back. "This was an excellent choice." I tried to put her in a better mood.

"Thanks," she said. "You have a knack for this sort of thing."

Max stood beside me and kept his silence.

She looked into the crowd, her eyes distant. Then they narrowed. "There's Mom and Dad."

They were mingling with a group of people, holding flutes and looking like royalty in their gowns.

"Should we go over there?" Ophelia's question was directed at Max.

"We have to face the music sometime." Max downed his glass then left it at the bar. "Let's go."

The three of us approached their group, and when they saw us, they didn't seem happy. Actually, they seemed a little surprised.

"Hey Mom and Dad," Ophelia said. Then she leaned and hugged them both.

"Hello," Victoria said. She returned the embrace but it was cold.

Max stared at them. "Hey." He hugged his mom but her affection was even colder.

His dad didn't reciprocate at all.

And they acted like I didn't exist.

The other couple they were talking to watched the interaction with interested eyes.

Man, this was awkward.

"Aren't you going to introduce us?" Max asked.

His mom regained her composure. "These are the Peterson's. We golf with them on the weekends from time to time."

"Pleasure to meet you." Max shook their hands. "I'm their son, Max."

"It's wonderful to meet you," they responded.

Then Max's parents introduced Ophelia.

I was left out. But I wasn't offended.

Max gave them a meaningful look. "And Jett?"

His mother pressed her lips tightly together before she spoke. "And this is Max's friend, Jett."

The shit was about to hit the fan.

"Actually, no," Max said. "Jett is my boyfriend."

His parents looked totally mortified and ashamed.

"Oh..." Mrs. Peterson nodded but her look was full of disdain. "How nice..." Her expression said it was anything but nice. Then they made an excuse to walk away.

It was clear how embarrassed his parents were.

Max glared at them venomously. "Parents are supposed to stand by their children no matter what, not be ashamed of them for who they are. You've both failed as parents." He turned away and marched toward the door.

Ophelia and I went after him.

Of course, his parents stood by and watched him go.

Max walked outside then moved down the steps. When he reached the fountain and the roundabout, he stopped. His hands were in his pockets but there was emotion in his eyes. He was broken by his parents' actions.

"Don't let them hurt you, Max," Ophelia said. "They're terrible people. But they'll come around."

Max was trying not to cry. "Give me a moment." He walked away then disappeared behind the trees.

For the first time I wasn't happy to be alone with Ophelia. I didn't care at all. All I could think about was Max, my friend, and how terrible he felt.

Ophelia crossed her arms over her chest. "He doesn't deserve to be treated like this."

"He doesn't…"

She sighed then shook her head.

"I'll be right back." I turned toward the trees.

Ophelia didn't try to stop me.

It was dark but I could make out a bench near the garden. A man sat alone—and he was crying.

I approached him slowly then took the seat next to him.

Max immediately withheld his tears and tried to act like he wasn't having a breakdown.

"You can cry," I said. "I don't think less of you or judge you."

He stared at the ground and kept his face averted.

I scooted closer to him then wrapped my arm around his shoulder. "I'm sorry about your parents. They shouldn't treat you like that and you don't deserve it."

He sniffed then wiped his tears away.

"But you got me. And you got Ophelia."

"You're only my friend because I'm paying you." His tone was dark.

"No, I genuinely care about you. I'm sorry if I didn't make that clear."

He stared down at his hands.

"I know this is hard but when people treat you like this, you need to cut them out. They are the ones choosing to miss out on things. There's nothing you can do. Maybe they'll realize they're wrong. Maybe they won't. But you can't let them tear you apart."

He was quiet for a long time. "But they're my parents…I love my parents."

"And I know they love you—even if they aren't showing it right now."

"I just want to be accepted, you know?" His voice was full of tears. "I'm the exact same person. I'm not any different. I just love men instead of women."

"I couldn't agree more. They'll realize that someday."

"All they care about is their image. Having a gay son is too embarrassing for them."

I rubbed his back. "One day, they'll realize all those snooty people in that room don't really care about them. It's all just a social act to increase their status. And they'll realize that their son does truly love them. They'll feel terrible for the way they treated you and they'll ask for your forgiveness. I promise."

"How can you make a promise like that?" he asked.

"I just can. I saw the way they treated you before you told them the truth. They adore both you and your sister. The news is just shocking to them."

He wiped his eyes on the sleeve of his jacket. "Crying is stupid…it's a waste of time."

"No. It's an expression of emotion. It's not stupid."

He took a deep breath then regained control of his faculties. "Thanks for making me feel better."

"No problem. It's what friends are for, right?"

"Yeah, I guess." He gave me a forced smile then looked at the ground.

Footsteps sounded behind us, and then Ophelia emerged from the shadows. She sat on the stone bench on the other side of Max. "Maybe you don't have Mom and Dad. But you always have me." She grabbed his hand and squeezed.

"I know, sis. I would never forget."

The three of us sat on the bench together, listening to the sounds of the party inside. But we seemed lost in a different world. Max was just a client but he quickly became something more. Now he was my friend, someone I really cared about.

And his sister was everything to me.

***

After we returned to the apartment, Max walked into his bedroom without saying good night. Judging his quiet dismissal, he wanted to be alone. I knew nothing I said or did would make this situation better so I decided to give him space.

Ophelia was clearly upset about it. She grabbed a beer out of the fridge then sat at the kitchen table as she drank it. She clearly didn't care how Cameron was doing anymore. She was miserable for her brother.

I sat across from her and slouched in the chair.

She drank half her beer before she abandoned it on the table. "Thank you for being supportive of my brother." Her voice barely came out as a whisper.

"You don't need to thank me for that. I care about him a lot."

"My parents are stupid…I'm starting to hate them."

I already hated them.

She ran her fingers through her hair in that sexy way she did everything but I was immune to it. I was hurting over my friend too much to care. Then she stood up and approached my chair.

I looked up at her, unsure what was going to happen.

Then she sat on my lap and wrapped her arms around my neck.

Instinctively, I pulled her closer to my chest and rested my chin on her shoulder. I hugged her tightly then pressed my face into her hair, inhaling her scent to keep me calm.

She felt right in my arms, perfect. Fortunately, I was depressed so my dick didn't come alive. Since she was sitting right on my lap she would feel it. She rested her head on mine while she remained quiet. We sat there together, feeling hopeless at the same time.

Caught up in the emotion, I pressed a kiss to her bare shoulder. I loved the way her skin felt on my lips. She tasted like sweet honey. I did it again because I couldn't control myself. I had a goddess in my arms and I wanted to worship her. Ophelia didn't seem to mind.

I finally controlled myself and stopped kissing her succulent skin. Instead, I held her while she felt feather light on my lap. Eventually, she buried her face into my neck and her breaths became deep and even. Judging the quiet sighs escaping her mouth she fell asleep.

I wanted to hold her all night but I knew that was a bad idea. She would get a kink in her neck from lying on me like this. And I wouldn't be able to stop myself from kissing the exposed skin in her dress.

I lifted her then carried her to her bedroom. After I lay her down, I pulled her heels off and tucked her into bed. When the sheets were pulled to her shoulder, she sighed happily like she was really comfortable.

I watched her sleep for a moment, wondering if I would ever sleep beside her until the morning came the following day. I wondered if she would ever hold me and tell me she loved me. I wondered if we would make love passionately and violently. I wondered a lot of things.

I leaned over her and pressed a gentle kiss to her forehead. I'd never done anything like that before, to any girl. It was a natural instinct. Then I tore my lips away so I wouldn't stay there forever.

"Jett..."

I turned back to her, loving the sound of my name on her lips. I stared at her and waited for her to say it again. But she didn't. I grabbed her hand and kissed her knuckles before I finally left her bedroom. Then I walked out, locked the door, and then threw her keys under the door into her apartment.

I leaned against the door and sighed, wishing I were in that bed with her.

Then my phone went off in my pocket. I wasn't in the mood to talk to anyone, but if someone was calling this late it must be important. I pulled it out and looked at the screen. It was Rhett.

"What?" I said when I answered. "I'm not in a good mood right now."

"Well, you're about to be." Excitement was in his voice.

"What's up?"

"We found something."

***

"What is it?" I asked as I entered Rhett's apartment. Cato was there too. They were both sitting at the kitchen table.

"Keep your voice down," Rhett said. "Aspen is sleeping." He pushed the paper toward me.

I sat down and snatched it. "What is this?" It looked like phone records. I scanned through the pages.

"We got his phone record from his service provider," Cato said. "It shows every call he made and…all his text messages." He gave me a knowing look.

"And if the number he's corresponding with isn't Ophelia's, then you got him," Rhett said.

My hands were shaking because I couldn't believe it. I started to look through it.

Want to come over?

Cameron responded. *Depends. What are you wearing?*

Nothing.

I kept skimming.

Dinner tonight? Cameron texted.

I want to try that new Italian place.

The messages reached back for the past three months.

"Is it Ophelia's number?" Rhett asked.

I pulled out my phone and compared. The truth hit me like a slab of bricks. I wasn't happy but I wasn't sad either. "No…"

Cato pounded the table. "Then you got that asshole by the balls."

I kept reading through the messages, unable to believe Cameron really cheated on Ophelia and for so long. The topics of their conversations were usually explicit, and it was clear they were sleeping together. And Ophelia was right. The owner of the orange bra was a slut.

"Go get her," Rhett said. "Why are you still here?"

I put the papers down. "Not so fast."

Cato groaned. "Now what do you want us to do? We have lives and wives, you know."

"You don't have a wife yet," I barked. "And I need to have Ophelia catch him in the act."

"Why?" Rhett demanded.

"Because if I throw this at her it'll make me look bad. If I take her somewhere where I know Cameron will be with this other woman, then I'm not the bad guy."

Cato sighed. "This girl better have the tightest pussy on the damn planet."

"Don't talk about her like that," I snapped.

He raised his hands in apology.

"Then what do you want us to do?" Rhett asked in a tired voice.

"I need you to follow him, and then when he goes out with this girl, you'll tell me and I'll bring Ophelia so she can see it first hand."

"That might be a problem," Cato said.

"Why?" I asked.

"Read the last few text messages," Rhett said.

I turned to the last page.

Cameron spoke first. *I told you I can't do this anymore.*

Why the hell not?

I'm going to try and make it work with Ophelia.

You said she was boring.

Cameron didn't respond for half an hour. *She wasn't always boring. I can make it work but I can't do that if I'm still seeing you. It's why the relationship went stale in the first place.*

Why am I not good enough?

Ophelia is marriage material. My parents like her, and I do want a family someday.

I stopped reading because I didn't need to keep going.

"It sounds like he's breaking it off," Rhett said. "You'll have a hard time catching them together."

I sighed and rubbed my temple. "Once a cheater, always a cheater. This girl is clingy so he'll have a hard time shaking her. And this conversation just happened yesterday. We have time."

Cato rubbed the back of his neck. "Dude, you owe us big."

"I know," I said. "If you help me bring him down, I'll do anything you want."

"Good," Rhett said. "Because I want you to wash my car every week for a lifetime."

"If I get Ophelia, that'll be a great trade," I said seriously.

"So, we'll stay on him and let you know what we find," Cato said.

"Record them together," I said. "Just in case I can't get her there in time."

"You got it," Rhett said.

I folded the papers then stuffed them into my pocket. I would use them if I had to but I'd rather not.

Chapter 6

Ophelia

Max was down for the next week. He didn't say much, and whenever I spoke to him it seemed like he was somewhere else. I tried to make him smile by telling him jokes or making breakfast and dinner.

Nothing seemed to help.

"I appreciate what you're trying to do," Max said. "But don't worry about me, Ophelia. I'll get over it."

I sat across from him at the table. "I just worry about you."

"Don't. I got Jett."

I was grateful he had a good guy in his life. Jett was thoughtful, loyal, and generous. He'd become one of my closest friends. Actually, he was my best friend. We did everything together and I felt like I could tell him anything.

When I wasn't with him, I missed him. I thought about him more than I thought about Cameron—by a landslide. Perhaps it was because Cameron and I hadn't really spent any time together. He kept getting sick or storming off.

I wished Jett would like him but it was clear he never would. While I liked having a friend who obviously cared about me, I wished they would get along. I was tired of being the referee in the middle of their fights.

I hadn't seen Jett that week and he hadn't texted me. I assumed Max was going to his place all the time so he could have some space. That was fine but I did miss him. I wished they would come over here. I could just text him but I wasn't sure if that was appropriate. I didn't want to be too clingy and irritate him. I already kissed him on accident and I was still embarrassed about it. He didn't make a big deal about it or make me feel guilty because he was a good guy. But I'm sure it made him uncomfortable.

I was at work and lunchtime had almost arrived when my assistant spoke through the intercom. "A gentleman by the name of Jett is here to see you, Ophelia. Shall I let him in?"

Butterflies the size of dragons swam through my stomach and I felt a little dizzy. Adrenaline pumped in my body then excitement. I wanted to jump out of my seat because I was so thrilled he was there. I quickly fixed my hair then checked my make up in the mirror but I wasn't sure why I did that. I never did stuff like that before. "Yes, send him in." I kept my voice professional because I knew Jett could hear me.

He walked inside then shut the door behind him. He wore dark jeans that hung low on his hips, and a gray t-shirt that made his body look amazing. His muscles were highlighted, and his biceps were appetizing. I wanted to squeeze them and I wasn't sure why. When I sat on his lap last week, I leaned against his hard chest and immediately fell asleep. Even though he was as hard as a rock, he was the most comfortable thing I sat on.

Unable to play it cool or sit still, I rose out of my chair then hugged him hard. I missed him and I couldn't hide it. A week without talking was a week without my best friend.

He returned the embrace with warmth. "Hey, sweetheart."

I loved it when he called me that. "I missed you."

He pulled away slightly and looked down into my face. "I missed you too." His eyes turned serious as he looked into my face. Then he leaned in and kissed me on the forehead.

The kiss burned my skin. I didn't even ask why he was there because I didn't care. All that mattered was the fact he was in my office—with me. I couldn't describe the connection between us but I knew it was there.

"I wanted to see if you wanted to get lunch." His hands were on my hips and he squeezed me gently.

"I'd love to," I said without hesitation.

"Great." He kept one hand around my waist as he opened the door for me and walked me out.

My assistant stared at Jett with obvious interest. Every woman checked him out like he was eye-candy. If only they knew he was gay. All the women in my office would break down in tears.

"What are you in the mood for?" he asked.

"Anything."

"Sandwiches?" he asked.

"Sure."

When we approached the deli, he opened the door for me, like always. Cameron never opened the door for me. Well, he used to years ago. Then he stopped. Recently, he started again. It seemed like he was only interested in doing things based on his mood.

We stood in line together and Jett stared at the menu. "What are you getting?"

"A cucumber sandwich."

He cocked an eyebrow. "Are you a rabbit now?"

"What if I am?" I challenged.

That cocky grin came over his face. "You're a cute rabbit then."

I smiled involuntarily.

After we ordered our food, Jett paid for it, like usual, and then we took a seat by the window.

He took large bites of his sandwich with that big mouth of his. He kept his elbows off the table, and his shoulders were so broad they extended past the chair.

I found myself staring at him longer than I should.

"How's your day going?" he asked.

"Good," I said. "Work is work."

"But you like it, right?"

"I love it."

"You should sneak me some t-shirts."

"What's your size?"

"Large, obviously." He wiggled his eyebrows at me.

I had to admit, I liked his cockiness. It never got old.

"I'll see what I can do. How's your day going?"

"Wonderful. I'm having lunch with a beautiful woman."

He was always so sweet to me, giving me more attention than anyone else ever had. "I was surprised to see you come to my office."

"Why is that?"

"You've never done it before."

He shrugged. "I just felt like it. I hope I can come more often."

"You can come whenever you want," I blurted.

He winked at me. "I will." He finished his sandwich then moved onto his chips.

I was suddenly aware of my body when I was around him. I felt anxious, almost nervous. I couldn't explain it.

"Want to come over tonight?" he asked. "I can cook dinner."

"What about Max?"

"Max is sick of me," he said with a laugh. "He needs space."

I wanted to, but I remembered I had plans. Disappointment filled me. "I can't…"

"Why not?"

"I'm going out with Cameron." I was actually bummed out I wasn't hanging out with Jett. Shouldn't I feel excited to see Cameron? He wasn't my boyfriend but that's where it was headed. Why did I want to spend more time with Jett, my gay friend?"

"Oh." Jett seemed just as disappointed. "I see."

It became awkward and I picked at my chips and kept my gaze downturned.

"You're wasting your time with him." His voice was suddenly aggressive. "He's no good for you."

I knew how Jett felt about him. He made it abundantly clear.

"Look at you, Ophelia. Supermodels like you need to be with a perfect man, nothing less."

I was flattered he thought so highly of me but I didn't deserve the praise.

"Dump him, Ophelia," he said. "Come on."

"Okay, I get it." I held up my hand because I knew he wouldn't stop until I silenced him.

"You're settling and I'm not going to let you settle."

"Jett, I don't want to argue about this right now."

He sighed but it came out as a growl. Then he looked out the window.

Maybe I should just end things with Cameron—for good. Would we ever be what we once were? Did we have any chance? The last few times I saw him the night ended prematurely. We hadn't even had a chance to kiss. And honestly, I wasn't sure if I wanted to.

He turned back to me, a serious expression on his face. "You need to promise me something."

"What?"

"Promise me you won't sleep with him tonight."

It was the weirdest request I ever heard. "Why?"

He leaned over the table and lowered his voice. "Just promise me. I can't tell you why. Just trust me."

"Uh…" I had no idea why he was asking me to do such a thing. Why did he care?

"Promise me," he pressed.

"Why are you making me promise such a thing?"

He sighed and closed his eyes. Then he reopened them. "I'm your friend, right? Maybe this is just on my part, but you're one of my closest friends. Do you feel the same way?"

"Of course I do."

"Then blindly trust me on this. I'll explain at a later time."

"You do understand how odd this is."

"Completely," he said seriously.

"Okay." I don't know why I agreed to it but I did.

"You promise?" he pressed.

"I promise."

He visibly relaxed.

"I wasn't going to sleep with him anyway. It's too soon for that."

"Then why didn't you just promise me to begin with?" he asked.

"I don't just do what someone tells me to do," I argued. "I'm not a mindless idiot."

"I'm glad to hear that," he said. "But you can be different with me."

I already had a feeling I was.

He looked out the window and remained in a somber mood. His eyes reflected the blue sky, and the colors were almost identical. A small amount of hair was growing on his chin and sides of his face like he hadn't shaved for a few days. His strong jaw caught my attention, like always. I wondered how it would feel to sprinkle kisses on it. His eyes shifted my way and he caught me staring at him.

But I didn't look away. I'd already been caught so I didn't see the point in pretending I wasn't watching him like a piece of artwork.

He didn't speak or make an arrogant comment like usual. Instead, he met my gaze without wavering. He didn't even blink. The deli was full of people having quiet conversations. Wrappers were open and then closed. People got ice in their cups from the soda machine. Trays were stacked on top of the trashcan. But all of those sounds seemed irrelevant. I could hear Jett breathe, and the sound was in tune to the rise and fall of his chest. Somehow, I could even hear his heartbeat.

And call me crazy, but I thought he could hear mine too.

***

Cameron picked me up then took me to an Italian restaurant in Manhattan. We sat across from each other at the table, and I realized this was the first time we'd really been alone together. It was awkward, and if I felt it, he must have felt it too.

He browsed his menu before he set it aside. "How's work?"

"Fine." There wasn't much to say. The highlight of my day was when Jett came to my office and took me to lunch. But I wouldn't say that to him. "How was your day?"

"We have another big case coming up. But it should have a big payout."

For the past five months, Cameron had been working hard on a criminal case. He'd worked nights and weekends, and we didn't see each other as often as I wanted to. "What happened to that other case you had?"

"What case?" he asked.

"The one you were working on all the time?"

"Oh." He nodded his head in understanding. "Uh…we won but now the defendant is trying to appeal it." His voice was different, high-pitched and uncomfortable.

Dangerous Stranger

What did I say to make him so uneasy? "Your stomach been giving you anymore problems?" It wasn't the best topic to bring up but I didn't know what else to say.

"Yeah, the bug lasted twenty-four hours then went away."

"Well, at least it was short-lived."

"How'd the benefit go?"

"Terrible," I said. "My parents treated Max like a dirty secret. We left within thirty minutes. And Max took it pretty hard."

He nodded but didn't say anything. It didn't seem like he cared much either.

"I'm glad he has Jett. He can be sensitive but firm at the same time."

A shadow fell over his eyes at the mention of Jett. The anger burned deep inside but he didn't voice his fury. "Spend a lot of time with him?" His tone was clipped, like he was annoyed.

"Yeah, we're friends."

"What do you two do together?"

"We go shopping…play board games…hit the gym. He's become one of my closest friends." It was hard to think about him and not smile.

"He's not gay."

He said this once before but I couldn't believe it. "He is."

"No, he's not."

"And why would he pretend to be gay with Max?" I asked. "He gets nothing out of it."

"I don't know," he said. "But he's not gay. I can tell. I've seen him check out your ass."

"He was probably checking out my dress."

"No, he wasn't," he spat. "I've seen him look at your chest."

"He may look at me but that doesn't mean he's checking me out."

"Am I the only one who sees it?" he asked incredulously.

"Apparently," I said coldly.

He rested his elbows on the table and surveyed the other people in the restaurant. His nostrils were flared.

"Gay or straight, what does it matter?"

"It matters because he's trying to get with you."

Jett wasn't trying to be with me. That wouldn't happen in a million years. "You're acting crazy."

He opened his mouth to argue.

"Are we here to talk about us or Jett's sexual preference?"

He closed his mouth again, but this time his jaw was tense.

The awkwardness was dissipated slightly when we ordered our food. I hoped the dishes would come soon so we'd have something to do other than look at each other. It was hard to believe there was a time when we were comfortable around one another. Now I didn't know him anymore.

"I know I wasn't the best boyfriend to you in the past year," he said quietly. "I intend to make up for that."

I sipped my wine and kept my silence.

"When you walked away, I had time to think about what you said. And I realized what my life was like without you. Sometimes you have to lose something to realize what you had to begin with…unfortunately."

I sipped my wine again.

"And when I thought about my future, you were the woman standing beside me. I want to have a house with you. I want to come home to you and my kids. I want a marriage."

Cameron had never mentioned it before but I assumed that was where our relationship was going.

"Now I know what I want. And I think we can make it happen if you forgive me."

"It's not something I can just forgive," I said. "Since it went on for so long…"

"I understand," he said. "I can be patient. You're worth the wait." He stared at me hard with the green eyes I once was fond of. Now they just reminded me of mold.

Thankfully, the waiter brought the food so I had something to do with my hands and eyes.

We ate quietly, and the constant clatter of silverware against the dishes reminded of the words we weren't speaking. It seemed as if neither one of us could think of something to talk about. But for the past few months of our relationship, we didn't do much talking. But we didn't do much fucking either.

When the tab arrived, I was grateful the evening was over. I just wanted to go home and spend the evening alone in bed. I didn't want to stare at Cameron across the table.

After the meal was paid for, we walked outside. Cameron grabbed my hand as we walked, and I let the affection linger even though it didn't feel right. His shoulder brushed mine as we walked back to my apartment.

"Your hand fits perfectly in mine," he said as he stared at them.

I glanced down but didn't agree.

When we arrived at my door, I had no intention of letting him inside. "Thank you for dinner," I said politely.

The stress in his eyes told me he knew this date wasn't going well. "Give me more time before you blow me off."

I crossed my arms over my chest.

"You know…I'm not really an emotional guy. I'm not good at explaining how I feel or showing it. I guess I'm a little nervous and scared. I want to fix this but it's hard when you're so closed off from me."

"I can't just change the way I feel, Cameron. I'm hurt. And I'll be hurt for a long time."

"And I understand that," he said quietly. "I'll be patient with you. But please be patient with me."

I was terrible when it came to patience. "I'll try." I grabbed my keys out of my purse and got the door open.

He grabbed me by the wrist but the touch was soft, not aggressive like Jett's was. He turned me toward him and leaned in.

Without thinking, I turned my face and gave him my cheek.

His lips pressed against my skin before they moved away.

I looked at him, feeling bad for rejecting him. "Good night."

He sighed in sadness. "Good night."

I walked inside then shut the door, relieved the solid barrier was between us. When I went to toss my purse on the table, I flinched when I spotted Jett sitting there. "Geez, you scared me."

"With my good looks?" he said with a smile. "Yeah, I catch everyone off guard with my pretty face."

I rolled my eyes even though I was amused.

Then he turned serious. "So, how'd it go?"

I shrugged. "It was fine."

"It doesn't seem fine."

"It's just...awkward." I ran my fingers through my hair to soothe myself.

"And you didn't sleep with him?" he asked.

"That's why you're here, isn't it?" I couldn't believe I didn't figure it out before.

"Not necessarily…"

I rolled my eyes again, but this time with meaning. "Good night, Jett." I headed to my room.

"Good night, sweetheart."

The nickname made me stop before my door. I gripped the handle but didn't turn it. Then I finally found my strength and walked inside.

***

I tossed and turned in my bed. The covers bundled around my legs and constricted me. I kicked them off then rolled onto my other side. My mind was in the middle of a dream, and I felt sweaty everywhere. My nightshirt clung to my back because it was moist.

Then the vision came to me, vivid and clear.

Jett moved on top of me, completely naked, and then cupped my face before he aggressively claimed my mouth with his. His tongue danced with mine then pulled out an involuntary moan against my will.

My hands glided over his body, feeling the mass of muscle and strength he possessed. My nails dug into him, wanting to keep him forever.

Jett yanked my clothes off, ripping them because he used such force. When I was naked beneath him, he wrapped my legs around his waist and entered me. "Sweetheart, I love you."

He felt so good when he stretched me. "I love you too."

He rocked into me slowly, making sweet love to me. He looked into my eyes as he moved. "Most beautiful girl."

My hands dug into his hair as I held on. "Jett…"

"I love it when you say my name."

"Jett," I repeated.

"I want you to say it when I make you come."

I felt the burn deep between my legs and then it burst like an inferno, making flames everywhere. I gripped him tighter then said his name over and over. "Jett…Jett…Jett." When the orgasm passed, I was suddenly aware of how hot I was.

My eyes flashed open and then I sat up in bed. The remains of the dream floated away and I tried to hold onto them, tried to remember how good it felt. Jett was there but I couldn't quite remember…

I went back to bed and forgot about the dream altogether.

Chapter 7

Jett

Ophelia didn't seem too happy at the end of her date, and when I looked through the peephole and watched them together, she gave him her cheek when he tried to kiss her. And she didn't invite him inside.

So that was good.

But it still irritated me she was dating him at all. What was a beautiful girl like her doing with a slug like him? I wasn't perfect but I could try to be—for her. She needed to let go of their old relationship and move on. It was done. If she knew he'd been cheating on her, she would walk away. But I really didn't want to throw it in her face and hurt her. It would be easier for me if she just walked away from the relationship. Then I wouldn't have to mention it at all.

But she was forcing my hand.

The guys were tailing him night and day, and so far, they didn't have anything to report. I knew Cameron would make his move and see his hussy again. If he weren't getting anything from Ophelia, he would go back to her even if it were just a quickie. I just needed them to meet somewhere in public. Then I could bring Ophelia and prove what a piece of shit he was.

The week went by and Cameron didn't do anything stupid. I was growing irritated. I could only keep Ophelia away from him for so long. I even asked Max to pretend he was still really depressed over his parents so she would stay home with him. Max must really like me if he was willing to do that. He wasn't convinced Cameron was cheating on her but I would get the proof no one could deny.

Then I finally got the call.

Rhett spoke over the line. "Sending something your way…"

"What do you got?" I asked.

"He's with a blonde at Staley's—it's a bar on 8th. Check your phone."

I stayed on the line with him and looked at the video he sent. It showed Cameron with a pretty blonde girl. They were making out near the bar, and it was clear it was him. The lighting was perfect. "You're the man!"

"I know I am," Rhett said. "But get your ass down here quick with Ophelia."

"I'm on it." I hung up then ran all the way to her apartment.

***

I banged on the door like a madman until she finally answered it.

"Damn, what's the emergency?" she said in an irritated voice.

"I need you to come with me—now."

"Where—"

"Just do as I say—please."

Hesitation was in her eyes.

"Just trust me, okay? I need to show you something."

She turned back to Max. "I'll be back in a little while."

Max eyed me. "Okay..." He probably knew why I was there.

"Then let's go." I snatched her wrist and pulled her out the door.

"What do you want to show me?"

"You'll see when we get there." I pulled her with me, making her walk so fast she was practically jogging.

"Why can't you just tell me?"

"It's hard to explain..." Actually, it wasn't that hard. We moved a few blocks then crossed the street. I would have waved down a cab but that would have taken longer. Almost out of breath, we finally reached the bar and I yanked her inside.

"A bar?" she asked. "Is this a joke?"

"Just come with me." I pulled her along with me.

Rhett was leaning against the wall with Troy.

"Where?" I asked.

He nodded toward the bar.

"Thank you." I pulled her with me.

Ophelia hadn't noticed them yet. "What's going on, Jett?"

I stopped until we were just a few feet away from Cameron and his blonde date. I turned to her, seeing the confusion in her eyes. She still hadn't noticed him. "Look to your right."

She cocked an eyebrow and did as I asked. Slowly, her face contorted and changed. Sadness crept into her features, along with disbelief. Her chest started to rise and fall at a quicker pace.

I hated watching it.

"That's him…"

I swallowed the lump in my throat. "Yeah…"

She continued to stare at them in shock. Soon, the sadness disappeared and was replaced by anger. Her eyes narrowed and a fire burned deep within. A man holding a beer passed her, and she snatched the glass out of his hand. "I just need to borrow this for a second."

I knew what was going to happen next.

She strutted to them, and while they were making out, she threw the drink in his face. "You lying piece of shit!"

Cameron broke apart from his girl and turned to her, wiping the beer out of his eyes.

"Gross!" The blonde stepped back.

When Cameron finally got his eyes cleared he looked at Ophelia in shock. It was clear he knew he was in deep shit and there was nothing he could do about it.

I stood behind Ophelia, and smiled and waved at him.

Ophelia smacked him hard in the face, and her hand moved so fast I didn't know she slapped him until she was finished. The people near him at the bar backed away. "You've been cheating on me with this slut? That was why the relationship fell apart? That was why you got bored with me? It was because you didn't have the stamina to handle two women." She slapped him again.

"Damn, " Troy said. "Don't piss her off…"

"All that bullshit about you wanting to marry me was just a joke," Ophelia said. "And I can't believe I was stupid enough to fall for it." Then she kicked him right in the balls and sent him falling to the ground. "Jackass."

She walked around him and headed to the exit.

I was torn. I wanted to kick Cameron's ass myself but I also wanted to be there for Ophelia.

"We got it," Rhett said, reading my mind. "When someone messes with one of our girls, they mess with all of our girls." He winked at me then gripped Cameron by the arm on the floor.

"Thanks, guys." I chased after Ophelia and saw her walking up the sidewalk. I jogged and caught up to her.

Her eyes were wet with tears but they didn't fall.

I felt no satisfaction for being right. Actually, I felt worse. "Sweetheart…"

"I'm so stupid," she hissed. "Such a stupid girl."

"You aren't stupid."

She kept walking and I had no idea where she was headed.

"He's just an asshole, Ophelia. Liars are hard to catch in the act because they've been doing it for so long. Just because you didn't know what he was doing doesn't make you at fault. It means you have a good heart and trust people."

"No, it means I'm a fool." She stopped on the sidewalk then turned toward a bar. "I need a drink."

I knew what she was going to do. "I have plenty of booze at my house. Let's go there."

"Yeah?" she asked.

"Yeah." I put my arm around her waist and walked her in the right direction.

She pushed away from my embrace. "I've never been so humiliated in my life."

"It wasn't your fault."

"All the signs were there. You even told me he was cheating and I didn't believe you…"

"That doesn't mean you deserve to be treated this way." I kept my voice gentle so I wouldn't make her more upset.

"I wasted two years of my life with that man."

"Not every relationship is meant to last. It usually takes a few relationships before you find the one. Just because Cameron didn't work out doesn't mean you're a bad partner."

She wouldn't look at me. "When he checked out that waitress like she was a damn porno star I should have known…"

I put my arm around her again. "Stop blaming yourself."

"Why?" she snapped. "I'm stupid and I know I'm stupid."

"Don't say that again." I pulled her tightly against me, telling her I meant business.

She felt silent and kept walking. But she looked in any direction that was opposite of me.

I finally got her to my apartment. The first thing she did when she walked inside was search my kitchen for booze. I'd never seen her act this way but I'd never seen her so upset either. I grabbed a bottle of patron and two shot glasses. "How about this?" I pulled out the chair for her and beckoned her to sit down.

She plopped down and immediately poured herself a glass.

I poured my own.

Then she clanked her glass against mine. "To hating men."

I drank to that then set my glass on the counter.

She cringed at the taste but kept it down.

I poured two more glasses. "Another round?"

"A million rounds."

She held up her glass and clanked it against mine. "Fuck relationships." She downed it just like the first.

I drank mine but pushed the bottle away. I could tell she was a lightweight based on her size. I didn't want her to be wasted in my apartment. She would feel worse the next morning.

"Another." She tapped her glass on the table.

"That's enough Ophelia." I kept my voice gentle.

She rested her elbows on the table and covered her face with her hands. "Ugh, I'm so dumb."

I scooted my chair closer to hers. "You aren't dumb."

"I'm a damn idiot. What the hell did I ever see in him?"

"Honestly, I don't have a clue." I hoped the humor would improve her mood.

It didn't. "I hate him. Honestly, I hate him."

"You should hate him."

"I hate him more than I've ever hated anyone." She lowered her hands and sighed.

"I think this is a good thing." I no longer held back. I gave her the affection I wanted without thinking about it. My hand cupped the side of her face, my fingers reaching her hair. "You were too good for him anyway. If he didn't value you as the gem you are, then it's good you aren't wasting another day with him."

She shook her head. "But I should have known…"

"No one ever knows these things. We should trust the person we're with and that's what you did. If anything, it makes him look worse." My fingers moved through her soft strands of hair. My face was close to hers, close enough for a kiss.

"Has anyone ever cheated on you?" she whispered.

I'd never been in a relationship before. But I couldn't tell her that. "Not that I know of."

"Well, it feels terrible…if you were wondering."

"I know how it feels," I said. "Because I feel what you feel right now."

She turned to me with watery eyes. "I shouldn't be so upset. I wish I wasn't so upset…"

"He betrayed you. It's perfectly okay to be hurt."

"But he isn't worth my pain."

"No, he's not." I agreed with that.

The tears finally fell and they broke my heart.

"Why couldn't he just have broken up with me? That would have hurt a lot less than this…when he was with me he was with her. He didn't respect me or care about me at all…he used me."

"And that's his mistake," I said. "It has nothing to do with you." I cupped her cheeks and wiped her tears away with the pads of my thumbs. Then I leaned in and kissed every drop of moisture, feeling the wetness on my lips and tasting the salt on my tongue. I kissed her everywhere, even the corners of her eyes. I wanted to soak up the pain for her. I wanted to carry the weight as my own. "You're every guy's fantasy, Ophelia. Don't let him make you feel otherwise." I continued to kiss her tears away, not letting any of them fall.

Her hands moved to my forearms and she gripped them as I held onto her. She didn't pull away or seemed uncomfortable by the affection. Her breathing increased and her fingers trailed across my skin. Finally, she stopped crying and looked at me with watery eyes.

I stared back at her, wondering what she was thinking. My fingers still touched her hair, feeling the softness. I wanted to kiss her, more than I ever had, but it would be unforgiveable to make a move now when she was vulnerable and upset. Somehow, I stayed away and remained a loyal friend.

"Can I sleep here?" she whispered.

"Of course you can," I said immediately. "I have extra bedrooms."

"I meant with you."

My heartbeat sped up. The blood pounded in my ears. "Yeah." I swallowed the lump in my throat.

She left the table and walked into my bedroom.

I watched her go, unable to believe I was finally going to hold her all night long. It would be better if it was under better circumstances but I would take what I could get. I followed her inside, and when I saw her looking through my drawers just in a thong I almost had a heart attack.

Her bare back was flawless. Her spine had grooves of muscle around it, and it was long and curvy. I knew her front would be just as sexy as her back. Her ass was perky and round, and seeing the black thong made my cock harder then a slab of wood.

Fuck, I don't know if I can do this.

She finally picked out a shirt and pulled it on. But she turned around when she was halfway covered and I saw her pierced belly button. A glittery jewel hung from her navel, and it was sexy as hell.

She got into my bed then pulled the covers over her.

I realized I was just standing there staring at her, so I pulled out thick sweatpants and changed into them, not wearing a shirt. At least the padding from my boxers and my sweatpants would hide my raging hard-on somewhat.

As soon as I was in the bed, she was all over me.

She cuddled into my side and wrapped her arm around my stomach. Her leg intertwined with mine and her hair moved across my arm. It would be a dream if she weren't so sad.

I pulled her further onto my chest and ran my fingers through her hair. I shifted my weight slightly so my boner wouldn't be poking her all night. My shirt was ten sizes too big for her so I moved it off her shoulder and sprinkled kisses there, just the way I always wanted. She didn't seem to mind. Actually, it seemed like she enjoyed it.

"You'll be alright," I whispered to her.

"I hope so…"

"You will. You got me, sweetheart."

"Why can't all men be sweet like you?" she asked. "Why can't they all be perfect like you?"

"You think I'm perfect?" I asked seriously.

"Why do you think I'm lying on your chest and clinging for dear life?"

My hand continued to stroke her hair. "Because you think I'm hot." I wanted to dissipate her sadness with laughter.

She chuckled lightly.

I was glad I got her to at least do that.

"You think everyone thinks you're hot."

"Because they do," I said. "Come on, look at me. I'm like an Abercrombie model."

"God, can your ego get any bigger?"

"I don't know," I said. "Want to find out?" I fisted her hair like I fantasized then pressed a kiss to her temple.

"I don't think it's possible. At least, I hope it's not possible."

My hand moved up her shirt and I felt her bare back. "Your skin is so smooth."

"Thank you."

My fingers graced the lace of her thong and I tried to act like I did it on accident. Did she really think I was gay? Did gay guys have their girlfriends come over and sleep on them like this? I'd never really asked so I wasn't sure. How she didn't see through my lie and know I was ridiculously attracted to her was beyond my understanding.

"I'm sorry I didn't listen to you," she whispered, her face on my chest.

"It's okay," I said. "I only had a hunch anyway."

"But you were right."

"It doesn't matter, sweetheart. All that matters is Cameron is gone and you can move on now."

"I guess..." Her voice carried her sadness.

"Is there something else?" I could detect it in her voice.

"Yeah...after we had dinner together I realized I didn't feel anything. I found it hard to believe that we would ever make something work between us. It just wasn't there...and I knew that. So, why am I so upset?"

"He still betrayed you," I said. "It would hurt anyone. And you guys were happy once upon a time. The fact he's pissing all over that is probably what gets under your skin."

"Yeah...maybe."

I wrapped my arm around her waist and let my hand rest in the dip of her back. It was such a sexy curve. I wanted to grace the area with kisses. I could touch it forever.

"Thanks for letting me sleep here."

"You're always welcome." *I meant it.*

"You're so comfortable to sleep on..." Her voice grew heavy, like she was tired.

"You like sleeping on hard pavement?" I teased.

"But you're warm…and you make me feel safe."

That touched my heart and I couldn't explain why. "I'll always keep you safe."

She turned her head and kissed the skin over my heart. "You're a gift, Jett. And I'm so glad we met."

Instead of closing my eyes, I watched her. She was an angel without wings. She had such a sweet and compassionate soul. She was generous and thoughtful, and she was hard when she needed to be. Even when she was at her lowest point, she was strong. I'd never met another girl like her. She was easy on the eyes and obviously beautiful, but now that I knew her underneath those beautiful curves I saw the gorgeous woman she was underneath.

And it made the rest of her pale in comparison.

***

When I woke up the next morning, she was still in the exact same place. She slept on my chest like a cat purring through the afternoon. Her hair was scattered everywhere and it felt soft on my skin. My hand still rested on the deep of her back.

I'd never woken up to such a beautiful morning.

My cock was hard like it usually was when I woke up, but now it was excited because we had beautiful company. I hadn't gotten laid in a while. The last time I slept with someone was the night before I met Ophelia. After I set eyes on her, I hadn't thought about anyone else.

That's how gorgeous she was.

Any girl could get my attention. But no girl could keep it. I wasn't even getting laid but I was obsessed with Ophelia. She was all I ever thought about. I wondered what she was doing throughout the day and if she was thinking of me. When I rubbed one out, I never turned on my laptop. Instead I thought about her sucking me off.

I was obsessed.

I had to pee, I was hungry, and I was thirsty, but I chose to stay still because of the beautiful creature lying on top of me. I didn't dare disturb her. I wanted to watch her wake up and see her reaction to me. I wanted to see those beautiful green eyes open and greet the day.

Finally, she stirred. She stretched her legs and her arms then released a deep sigh. Then she moved her hand across my chest before her eyes fluttered open.

I watched the whole thing, entranced by something anyone else would find boring.

When her eyes focused on me, a nice smile broke out on her face. "Good morning."

"Morning, sweetheart." Without thinking, I cupped her face and leaned in to kiss her. I quickly realized what I was doing, that I was about to do something I could never take back, and aimed for her cheek instead of her lips.

Phew, that was close.

She released another sigh when she felt me. "You're more comfortable than my own bed."

"I get that a lot," I teased.

She sat up then untangled her hair with her fingers. Then she looked down at me, saw my naked chest, and then quickly turned away. "At least I slept well."

"I did too." I sat up and pulled her against my chest. "But I think it's because I had my own teddy bear." I pulled her shirt down again and kissed her shoulder. Now I wasn't even bothering to act gay. She was totally clueless.

"I'm soft and fluffy?" she asked.

"And so cuddly," I whispered. Her shoulder was in my mouth again and I tasted her skin. "How about some breakfast? You like pancakes, right?"

"Do you not know me at all?"

"Then let's get some grub."

We went into the kitchen and started cooking. She took care of the pancakes while I flipped the bacon. She only wore my t-shirt and it fit her like a dress. It reached past her knees and it was baggy. But she still looked damn fine in it.

She nudged me in the side while she cooked, a playful smile on her lips.

I nudged her back then shoved an entire pancake into my mouth.

"Hey, you're supposed to wait until we're done."

"Whatever you say, sweetheart." I stuck my finger in the bowl of batter then wiped it across her cheek, smearing it. "Now you look perfect."

She tried to reach the batter with just her tongue but it wouldn't reach.

"Don't pull a muscle," I teased.

"I like it there anyway."

When we finished cooking, we sat down and ate everything. I was still shirtless and I caught her looking at me a few times. In the beginning, I wasn't sure if she was attracted to me, but the longer I was around her I suspected she was. I caught her staring at me, and it took all my strength not to break down, throw Max under the bus, and just tell her the truth.

"This bacon is so crispy." She took a bite and it cracked into several pieces. "You did a good job."

"I'm amazing in bed but I'm also amazing in the bedroom."

Her cheeks blushed slightly but she didn't say anything.

We finished our meal and left the pile of dirty dishes in the sink.

"So, how are you feeling today?" I asked. My meaning was implied.

"A lot better," she said with a sigh. "It's stupid to be upset over someone who never really cared about me, especially when I have people who do care about me." She shot me a smile then looked away.

If only she knew how much I did care about her. "What do you want to do today?"

"With you?" There was a slight note of surprise in her voice.

"Obviously," I said. "I'm the coolest person you know. Why wouldn't you want to hang out with me?"

"The cockiness never ends…" She shook her head slightly.

"There's this new action film I want to see. You down?"

"*You down?*" she repeated. "Am I one of your homies?"

"Yes," I said simply. "Then we'll get some greasy food and eat it in front of the TV."

"Actually, that sounds pretty damn amazing."

"Well, I know how to make a girl have a good time."

"Do you have other girlfriends?"

"No," I said immediately. "Just you."

"Really?" She seemed surprised by that. "Max has a few."

I shrugged. "I just don't. Do you have a lot of guy friends?"

"No…"

"It's not so weird now, huh?" I left the table. "I'm going to shower then we'll be on our way."

"Okay."

"Unless you would like to shower first?"

"No, it's okay," she said quickly.

"Or watch me shower…?" I gave her my usual grin.

She threw a pancake at me. "Get over yourself."

***

We got a bowl of popcorn from the concession stand then took our seats. My phone vibrated the moment we sat down, and I quickly checked it.

Did my sister stay with you last night? It was Max. *She never came home last night and Cameron showed up at the door demanding to see her.*

She's with me. Why didn't you just call her?

Her phone is off.

Oh. Well, she's fine.

K. Thanks.

I put my phone back in my pocket. "Next time you turn off your phone tell your brother where you are."

"I totally forgot…"

"Remember next time. Luckily for you, he assumed you were with me."

She grabbed a handful of popcorn and shoved it into her mouth. "Where else would I be?"

***

After the movie, we grabbed burgers and fries and headed back to my place. We sat on the couch and ate everything, acting like pigs that couldn't care less.

"Open your mouth." I held up the fry like I was going to throw it in her mouth.

She opened wide.

I tossed it into her mouth and made it. "Score."

"I'm a pro. My brother and I do this with jelly beans all the time."

"You should quit your day job," I teased.

She laughed. "Never. I love my job too much."

"So, you want to sleep over again?" I asked hopefully. I wasn't tired but I wouldn't mind lying in bed with her. While I loved hanging out with her and going out, I loved just holding her in bed. It was peaceful.

"No…I should probably head home."

I tried not to act devastated. "Okay. You're always welcome if you change your mind."

"I would love to but I have work in the morning."

"I could stay with you…" It was a dangerous suggestion and I probably shouldn't have said anything.

"No, it's okay. You've taken care of me enough as it is."

I'll take care of you forever. "At least let me walk you home."

"Like you would take no for an answer anyway."

***

I walked her inside then grabbed her by the arm. "Let me know if Cameron bothers you. I'll scare him off like a damn scarecrow."

"Well, that might not work because he's not a bird…" Her lips pulled up in an involuntary smile.

"Oh, it'll work."

She suddenly shifted her weight and looked at the ground. "Thanks for being there for me…I really appreciate it."

"I'll be here—for anything." I hugged her and held her close.

Max came out of his bedroom and headed our way. His hands were in his pockets as he watched us. He shook his head slightly, like he knew exactly what I was thinking while I held his sister.

She pulled away then turned to Max. "Hey, sorry about last night."

"It's okay," he said. "So, you and Cameron had a fight?"

"Actually, we broke up. I caught him cheating on me, and it's clear he's been cheating for a while," she said.

"Oh." He looked disappointed. "I'm sorry."

"It's okay," she said with a smile. "I got my two boys." She grabbed both of our forearms before she walked into her bedroom and shut the door.

Max sighed. "You were right?"

"Yeah."

He scratched the back of his head. "I'll take care of him."

"My boys already did."

He nodded. "That explains all the bruises and swelling when he came over here. I thought he got mugged or something."

"No."

"Well, at least he's gone. That's something to be grateful for."

I couldn't live in this lie anymore. I couldn't handle it for a second longer. I was tired of pretending to be something I wasn't. Ophelia and I had something and she needed to know the truth. "Let's go for a walk."

***

We sat on the stairs outside the apartment building and watched people pass on the streets.

"What is it?" Max asked, leaning against one wall. His body was directed my way but his head faced the street.

"Let me tell her the truth," I said. "I can't keep lying anymore."

He sighed and looked away.

"Max, I'm in love with her." I never said it out loud before but I knew it was true. I could feel it every time I looked at her. When she cried in my arms, I wanted to cry too. "She needs to know how I feel. And call me crazy, but I think she might feel the same way."

"She thinks you're gay."

"I know...but there's something there."

He wouldn't look at me.

"Max, please. I'll still do as you ask for your parents. Why can't I just tell Ophelia? She'll keep your secret."

"You aren't as bright as I thought."

"Then enlighten me, "I said darkly.

"If Ophelia dates you, people will see you together, including my parents. How do you think that makes me look? You were gay and now you're straight? It'll be even more difficult for me to get them to accept me."

"Well, she and I can keep it a secret."

"People will see you together," he hissed. "And Cameron will be the first person to rat you out. He's close with my parents. Dude, it can't happen."

He was stabbing me in the gut. "Max, I'll beg if I have to."

"You'll just have to wait until this is over."

I didn't want to say these words but I had to. "What if it's never over? What if they never let it go?"

He stared at his shoes. "I need to give them more time. It's only been a few months. They might come around."

"Well, how long are you going to wait?"

"I don't know," he said with a shrug. "Six months?"

There's no fucking way I'll be able to keep my hands off her for another six months. It was a miracle I kept my hands to myself this long. "Please help me out. I really love your sister. I'm not going to be a dick to her like Cameron was."

"And I'm not worried you will be," he said simply. "But that has nothing to do with it. If you really want this, there's nothing stopping you. I can't control what you do. The contract even states you can end the arrangement for any reason whatsoever. Then end it if you must." He watched the people pass on the sidewalk.

I ground my teeth in irritation. "I'm not going to throw you under the bus."

"Then I guess everything will stay the same."

I wanted to scream. "You aren't even willing to compromise with me on this?"

"No." He finally looked at me. "How will it make me look if my first boyfriend was gay and then became straight in the middle of our relationship? It would give people more to talk about, and my parents would think I'm a bigger freak than I already am. I hired you because I thought you were professional. I thought you could handle this. I guess not." He looked away but his shoulders were tense in anger.

"Max, I will do as I promised. I just…"I rubbed the back of my neck. "I've never felt this way about someone before. I feel like she's already mine…just not officially."

"I don't know what to say. I told you to stay away from my sister."

"And you should have known how impossible that would be."

Chapter 8

Ophelia

As the days passed, so did my sadness. What was the point in being upset over someone else's actions? Our relationship had been falling apart for a while, and I made the right decision when I decided to end it.

And I should have stuck to my guns.

Instead, I gave him another chance when I knew in my heart I shouldn't have. I kept living in the past, remembering the good times we had and what a great man he was. But those times were long gone.

Now I paid the price for my foolishness.

But Jett made it much better. He spent time with me when I knew he had better things to do. He went with me to the gym and took me out for ice cream. We were attached at the hip like close friends.

When I wasn't with him, I wish I were. I felt bad I was hogging Jett so much. I apologized to my brother countess times but he didn't seem to care. Their relationship was odd. Sometimes it seemed like they were into each other, but a lot of the time, they seemed almost indifferent.

I was thinking about the lava cake we made at Jett's apartment the night before when my assistant spoke over the intercom. "Cameron is here to see you."

My blood suddenly turned cold. He'd been blowing up my phone constantly, and I never listened to all the voicemails he left. His pathetic apologies and explanations meant nothing to me. "Send him away."

"I don't think I...sir, you can't go in there!"

I knew he was barging in my office whether I wanted him to or not. My workday was almost over anyway so I decided to clock out a few minutes early. I snatched my purse and phone then walked around the desk.

Cameron walked inside, his face slightly pink from old bruises and cuts. "Listen to me." He held up his hand like that would stop me.

I held my phone just the way Jett taught me, so I could hit him right in the nose with the butt of it. "Get out of my way."

"Just give me a chance to explain what happened."

"I saw you sticking your tongue down her throat," I snapped. "There's nothing left to explain."

"No, it's not like that."

I rolled my eyes because his excuses were more pathetic than I thought they would be. "Go to hell." I walked out of my office and took the stairs. I wanted to get out of there as quickly as possible and attract the least amount of attention. Cameron was close behind me the entire time but he didn't cause a scene.

Once I was out of the building, I turned left and headed to Crunch Fitness like I did every day after work. Jett was usually there early. As soon as I saw him I knew I would feel better about this creep riding my ass.

"Ophelia!" He jogged to catch up to me. "Just listen to me for five minutes, okay?"

"No." I kept walking, acting like he didn't exist.

"I'm going to keep harassing you until you give me a few minutes. So, keep running or stop and give me your attention."

I couldn't argue with his logic. If I gave him what he wanted, he might leave me alone. I stopped then put my hand on my hip, giving him the nastiest glare all the popular chicks in high school taught me. "You got two minutes—go."

"When we were first together, everything was great. I was happy and you were happy. Then we both started working more and we just drifted apart. That's when I met Elena—"

"I don't care what her name is."

He kept going. "Things just happened, and before I knew it...we were in a relationship."

At least he was being honest. I was surprised he offered that.

"That was why you and I drifted apart. That was my fault. What I did was wrong and I shouldn't have made that mistake. You're an amazing girl and I was just stupid. When you dumped me, I realized what I lost. So...I ended it with her so I could be with you." He gave me a hopeful look. "And only you."

That's what he wanted to say? "So...since you tried breaking it off when we got together I'm supposed to be impressed by that?"

"I know I made a stupid mistake and I learned from it."

"I caught you making out with her!"

"I was breaking up with her," he argued. "And you and I weren't together anyway."

That just made my head explode. "Excuse me?"

He cringed like he knew the mistake he made.

"Oh..." I clutched my heart with emotion. "How sweet. I can't believe you did that for me, baby." Then I gave him another glare before I walked off.

"Wait." He grabbed me by the wrist, and this time he used all his force to keep me still. "I want another chance—a real one."

I kicked him in the groin but he blocked it. "Your two minutes are up, asshole."

"I said I was sorry. It won't happen again."

I got in his face. "Even if I believed you, which I don't, I don't want you anymore." I tried to twist away from his grasp.

"Because you're in love with a gay man?"

My eyes widened in offense. "What if I am?" I don't know what possessed me to say that but it came out.

"You call me a cheater but you've been running around with pretty boy all over town."

"But I wasn't sleeping with him." I tried to push him off. "Now let me go."

"No. I'm not done talking to you." He squeezed me harder and pulled me to his chest.

I tried to kick him again but he kept blocking his testicles. "You fucking dick!"

"Let her go." His commanding voice made me stop fighting. It moved down my spine and made me feel scared but safe at the same time.

Cameron loosened his hold when he realized he had company.

Jett stood a few feet away, his arms hanging by his sides. Threat was in his eyes, and he looked a little crazy. "Let her go or I'll make you."

He finally let me go, loosening his grip on my wrist.

"Smart choice." Jett grabbed me and pulled me behind him. Then he dropped his gym bag and approached Cameron with the obvious intent to kick his ass. "No one touches my girl and gets away with it." Quicker than I could see, he jabbed him in the nose then the jaw. Cameron was on the pavement, wiping the blood away.

I didn't defend Cameron this time. He deserved it.

"I guess my friends didn't teach you a lesson." He rolled up his sleeves.

Cameron scrambled to his feet then took off at a dead run.

Jett stood there and watched him go. "Pussy." His shoulders were tense, and he breathed hard like he might decide to chase after him. When he made up his mind to stay put, he turned back to me. "Are you alright?" His hand snaked around my waist like it belonged there.

"Yeah, I'm fine."

He grabbed his bag and walked with me. "Want to skip the gym today?"

"Sure."

"A drink?"

A glass of scotch sounded nice right now. "Please."

We walked into the closest bar, the one I happened to catch Cameron in, and then sat in a booth. Jett got the drinks then sat down again. Like we were in a western, he slid the glass to me across the table. "Bottoms up."

I took a drink but I could only manage that—a drink.

"So, what happened?" He tilted his glass and the ice cubes slid around.

"He came to my office and said he wanted to explain what happened."

"I think it's pretty self-explanatory." His eyes held his anger, and his body held his rage.

"I said the same thing. But he wouldn't leave my office so I left instead. Of course, he followed me. I gave him two minutes to explain himself. Actually, what he said was pretty funny…"

"Which was?" He leaned over the table while he listened to me.

"That he was cheating on me but he stopped so he could give this relationship a real chance. Apparently, I'm marriage material and she's not." I made a sympathetic look with my face. "Isn't that the sweetest thing you've ever heard?"

He laughed as he took a drink. "They should have put that plot in Titanic."

I rolled my eyes. "I'm hurt about everything but I'm also angry. I just feel stupid."

"Like I said, you shouldn't feel that way."

"Too late." I drank the rest of my glass and felt the burn all the way down my throat. "I'm going to get another."

"Whoa…hold on." He held me in my seat with just his eyes. "It's the middle of the day and alcohol won't solve your problems. One is enough."

I stuck my tongue out at him. "You're no fun."

"I'm responsible. And I take care of you."

"Still boring," I teased.

"Hey, I'm a very adventurous guy. But I'm also a protective one."

"You don't say?" I snatched his drink and downed it.

His lips twitched in an involuntary smirk. "I'll let that go since you're cute."

"You'll let that go because you know I could take you."

"Only because I would let you," he said. "You want to do something tonight?"

"Like what?" I spent most of my time with Jett. He was starting to feel like home. I'd neglected all my other friends since he came into my life. And my brother didn't care but it was probably because he knew I was going through a hard time.

"A paint club."

I cocked an eyebrow.

"It's where you drink and play drums while paint gets all over you."

"Sounds like a big mess."

"It'll be fun," he said. "It'll get your mind off of it."

"Sure," I said. "I'll do anything with you because you're the only person I want to do anything with."

His teasing smirk disappeared, and his eyes softened in emotion. "The feeling is mutual."

***

My friends found out about Cameron and I through the grapevine. What grapevine? I wasn't sure. But they knew. And naturally, they wanted to go out and hear the tale. But they picked a loud bar full of people dancing and having a great time. It was hard to hear myself speak.

"Then I caught them together at a bar," I finished.

Denise looked like she wanted to snap someone's neck—anyone's neck. "That sleazebag. He didn't deserve you to begin with, and then he treats you like that…" She shook her head in disgust. "Terrible."

"Yeah." I went onto my fourth drink and felt the buzz shift into something deeper.

"You slapped him good, right?" Jasmine asked.

"As hard as I could. But Jett took care of him—a few times, actually."

"Jett?" Denise asked.

"He's my friend," I said. "Actually, he's my brother's boyfriend." It was still weird to think about. I was closer to Jett than I was to my own brother. We did everything together, even slept together.

"Gay men are the best," Jasmine said. "Truly."

"Yeah, and he's so damn hot." I blurted that out when I shouldn't because I was drunk. "Why do gay men have to be so fine? He's like the hottest guy I've ever seen."

Denise raised an eyebrow. "Are you crushing on your brother's man?"

"No," I said immediately. "Of course not. But he is really hot. You should see him."

"I don't want to be tempted," Jasmine said. "If I can't have him, then why torture myself?"

I could say the same thing.

"You're getting laid tonight," Denise said. "By a fine guy who knows what he's doing."

Dangerous Stranger

I wasn't interested in hooking up with a random stranger. I'd rather sleep with Jett and listen to him cheer me up. I never participated in the hook up culture even before Cameron came along. "I'm okay."

"Come on," Jasmine said. "At least talk to a cute guy."

I finished my drink and moved onto a fifth. Like the alcohol suddenly had its affect, I drifted into a haze and felt the lack of inhibitions. I was so angry with myself for letting Cameron fool me, and I hated him for hurting me. I just wanted to drift away for the night and not rely on my brother's ridiculously hot boyfriend to make me feel better. The thought made me realize just how strange my life had become. "Okay. What the hell?"

Denise clapped her hands in excitement. "That's my girl."

***

Denise and Jasmine found guys to entertain them for the night, and a decent looking blonde guy came my way. He smiled and had charming things to say, but I was so drunk I could have been talking to a manly girl and wouldn't have known the difference.

My head was starting to pound from drinking too much but he kept buying me more rounds. "You're in fashion?" he asked.

"Yeah, I'm an assistant chief editor."

"Pretty cool," he said. He pushed the drink closer to me. "That doesn't surprise me. You have good taste in clothes."

I couldn't remember what I was wearing. A black dress? I looked down and it still didn't register.

He leaned close to me, close enough for a kiss. "Want to head to my place?"

He was cute but I wasn't interested in sleeping with him. I never put out on the first day anyway, especially with a random dude. "No, I have to get up early tomorrow..." *What was tomorrow anyway? Tuesday?*

"Come on." His hand moved to my thigh. "My bed is really comfortable. You can sleep over."

I decided to hit the bathroom. I thought I might throw up. I should have drunk water along the way like a smart person. "I need to...pee..." I got out of the chair and wobbled a little bit.

"Whoa, there." He grabbed me and steadied me. "You can use the bathroom at my place."

"No, I'd rather just go here..." I pushed through the crowd and felt him right behind me. When I got to the bathroom he grabbed me and pushed me against the wall.

"You trying to run away from me?" There was a teasing note to his voice but he also seemed serious.

"No, I just..."

His lips sought my neck and began to kiss me. His hands move to my boobs and he groped them in public.

Dangerous Stranger

I needed to get away from this guy. I shoved him off but I was weak.

"Loosen up," he said. "Are you always this uptight?"

I managed to move past him and enter the bathroom. But I was wobbling and barely in charge of my faculties. I was Bambi in heels. I was too weak to make it to a stall so I leaned against the wall then slid to the floor. Girls checked their make up in the mirror and washed their hands. They all ignored me.

I knew the guy would come in here for me eventually if I didn't come out. There was no window for me to crawl out. Luckily, I have my clutch so I opened it and searched for my phone. Everything was blurry and my hands were shaking. I managed to find Jett's name and hit send.

Chapter 9

Jett

I was looking over a folder for a new client when Ophelia called me. Her name flashed on the screen, and like always, my heart hammered in my chest. She wasn't my girlfriend, she had no idea I was straight, and she had no idea I was head-over-heels for her, but it felt like she was mine. I swiped my thumb across the screen then answered the call with a smile. "Missed me?" I made my voice sound as arrogant as possible.

"Jett?" Her voice sounded unusually high-pitched and weak. Loud sounds were in the background, people talking and distant music. And she sounded sick, like she was about to throw up in a toilet.

"Baby, what's wrong?" My heart sped up, and not in a good way, and I suddenly felt faint.

"Please come get me…" She breathed hard like she was in pain.

I was on my feet instantly. "Where are you?"

"I don't know…" She sounded scared. "I'm in a bar and there's this guy outside. Shit, I'm so drunk. I can barely see."

What guy? She was wasted? Now I was terrified. "What bar?"

"I can't remember…"

I was walking out the door and grabbing my keys. "Think, baby. Come on. I'll search every bar in Manhattan but give me something to work with. What stores are around it? What street is it on?"

"Uh…"

I wanted to scream. I had to get there before this creep got to her. "THINK!"

"Our gym is just down the road." Her voice sounded muffled, like she was moving.

"Okay." That gave me something to work with. I kept her on the phone as I jogged down the street. "Give me something else. What does the name of the bar start with? An A? An R?"

"Uh…" She said a few incoherent words.

"Concentrate," I reminded her. The idea of some asshole touching her was making my temples hurt.

"Riso's…Rizo's…Ricos…"

"Rizzo's?" I felt triumphant for figuring it out.

"Yes!" Her voice didn't sound weak for the first time.

I would be able to run faster without her on the phone. "I'm going to hang up. Stay in the bathroom. Do not walk out of there. You understand me?"

She sounded far away. "Yes."

"I'll be there in a few minutes. Just hold on."

"Okay."

I hung up without saying goodbye then took off at a sprint.

***

I cut in front of the line and pulled out all the cash I had. "Look, my girlfriend is drunk off her ass in there and some guy is about to snatch her. Let me pass." I pulled out two hundred and eighty five dollars. "Please let me in."

The guy eyed the angry people standing behind me then discreetly took the money. Then he unclipped the rope and let me pass.

"Thank you!" I clapped him on the shoulder as I ran. Once I was inside, the lights were low and the floor was crowded. I pushed through people until I could spot the bathrooms. There were two different sets. I didn't have time to pick the wrong one.

I debated for a moment before I dashed to the one to the left. Not caring about anyone in the world than Ophelia, I pushed past the girls in line, listening to them hiss and complain, and then made it inside. "Ophelia!" I looked around but didn't see her anywhere. I banged my fist on every stall but she didn't respond. All I got was, "Get the hell away, asshole!"

Dangerous Stranger

She must be in the other one. I hightailed it out of there and pushed through the crowd once more. I was pretty sure I knocked a drink out of a guy's hand but I moved so quickly he didn't see where I went. I stormed toward the other bathroom when I heard a woman's voice.

"Leave me alone." The voice was weak and pathetic, like it was too difficult for her to form complete sentences.

I stopped and turned, hoping it wasn't her.

A man had his arm around a brunette's waist and he was dragging her through the room without actually picking her up. He looked like a sleazebag. It was written all over him. And I identified Ophelia in his arms.

She was practically being dragged across the floor. Her hair was in her face, and she wore a short, tight black dress. It was riding up, almost revealing more than just her thighs.

I saw red.

I grabbed the guy by the shoulder, and using more strength than I thought I could muster, I slammed him hard against the bar.

Ophelia was released and she wobbled on her feet.

"Baby, I'm here." I scooped her into my arms and cradled her to my chest.

She held her clutch weakly. "Jett?"

"It's me. I got you."

The asshole got to his feet and looked like he was about to come after me. "Get your own girl."

I knew I should walk away but I couldn't. I kicked him hard in the kneecap, making him scream as he fell to the floor again.

I knew I had to get out of there fast. I caused enough of a scene and there might me legal consequences unless I left without showing my face. I pulled Ophelia closer to my chest and carried her out the door.

The bouncer raised the rope and let me leave without question.

Once I was on the sidewalk and the club was behind me, I relaxed. Ophelia was safe in my arms and nothing happened. She was okay, so I was okay.

"Jett?" Her arms were around my neck.

"I'm taking you to my place. We'll be home soon."

"Okay…"

She was feather light in my arms, like an easy workout at the gym. Her scent came into my nose, and her perfume calmed me. I was grateful she called me to get her. I didn't trust anyone else to get her out of there safely.

When we reached my apartment, I got her inside and placed her on my bed. She looked up at me with lidded eyes. Her dress rode up past her thighs, and if I looked down I'd probably see her underwear. But I kept my eyes on hers.

Her hair was styled and shiny, and heavy make up was on her face. She looked like a bombshell. It didn't surprise me some guy preyed on her weakness. He would never get another chance with a girl nearly as hot.

"You can rest now," I said. "We'll talk in the morning." I was a little pissed off she got so drunk that she couldn't walk. I knew she was upset about what happened with Jett, but putting herself in danger was unacceptable.

"Thank you for taking care of me," she whispered.

"I'll always take care of you." I said it without thinking.

She stared into my eyes like she was going to say something.

I stared back at her, waiting for something to happen.

Then she gripped my shirt and pulled me on top of her.

Before I knew it, her lips found mine and she kissed me—hard. Her fingers moved through my hair and she breathed hard into my mouth. Then her tongue made an entrance and burned me in such a good way.

The kiss was nothing like I expected. I'd fantasized about it so many times, and it was never this good. She kissed me like she loved me, like she couldn't live without me even if she tried. Her legs moved around my waist, and we were locked in a tight embrace.

Being human, I kissed her back and gave her everything I had. I cupped her face as I kissed her, feeling our lips smack together in a heated embrace. Our tongues danced together like they'd done this before. Then I sucked her bottom lip and released a moan.

"Jett…"

She was making all my dreams come true.

Then she unzipped her dress and pulled it off.

I knew what she was doing, was totally aware of it, and I didn't stop it.

She wasn't wearing a bra, and her tits were revealed to me. They were voluptuous and perky. Her nipples were hard like she was cold, and they looked absolutely delicious. I stared at them with a dropped jaw, unable to stop.

She got her dress off then yanked my shirt off.

I didn't stop her either.

Then she kissed me again as she removed my jeans and boxers.

I was aware of how naked I was, that my hard cock was there for her to see.

Then she pulled me back on top of her and our lips found each other again. As I lay on her, I felt my cock press against her stomach. My hand fisted her hair and I kissed her aggressively, telling her she was mine, and not just for the night. I gripped her black thong then pulled it down her legs, getting her ready for me to take.

She kissed me harder and wrapped her legs around my waist. "Jett…"

I broke apart then pulled a tit into my mouth. I sucked the nipple and moaned at how good she felt. I groped the other breast then pinched the nipple slightly. She was so beautiful that I couldn't process it.

Then I realized what I was doing.

I was a fucking asshole.

I rescued her from a creep that wanted to do the same thing to her.

And now I was doing it to her, taking advantage of her when she was drunk out of her mind.

This was the woman I loved.

I had to stop.

It took all my strength to move off her. I moved back, out of breath and hard as hell.

She reached for me, like she didn't want me to go. "Jett…" She gripped my shoulders and pulled my lips to hers again.

Goddammit. Just a few more kisses. I grabbed her neck while I kissed her passionately. Our tongues moved together, and I wanted to make her moan by slipping inside. But then I managed to break apart again.

"Come here," she said with a sexy voice.

I deserved a purple heart for this. "In the morning."

"I want you know."

This woman was killing me. "In the morning." It was all I could say.

She looked at me with disappointed eyes. They were full of alcohol and emotion.

Stay strong, Jett. I'd never forgive myself if I took her under these circumstances. She wouldn't even remember it the following morning. I wanted her, but not like this.

If I covered her, it would make this easier. I grabbed a t-shirt then pulled it over her head and covered her gorgeous tits and endless curves. "Let's get some sleep."

She didn't pull the shirt off but she didn't look happy.

I grabbed her thong off the floor and resisted the urge to inspect it in detail. I pulled it up her beautiful legs and covered her, doing my best not to stare at the area between her legs. *Believe me, I wanted to.*

I pulled my boxers on then got into bed beside her. My arms enveloped her in a loving embrace and I held her close.

She was distant with me. "You don't want me..."

I pulled her against my chest and kissed her forehead. "I do want you. But not like this."

Her arm hooked around my stomach. "I...I'm sorry." Her words started to grow faint and sound incoherent.

"Don't apologize."

"I don't know what happened...I drank too much."

She was making less sense. "Go to sleep, sweetheart. We'll talk in the morning."

She took a deep breath and released a sigh. "Okay..."

***

She slept in late the next day. I woke up at nine but she slept passed noon. Unable to lay in bed with her because I had a full bladder and I was starving, I moved from her arms then went into the kitchen. After breakfast and coffee, I watched a game on the couch.

I kept checking the time, wondering when she would wake up. When I got worried, I checked on her to make sure everything was okay. She was sleeping peacefully, her body wrapped around a pillow like she thought it was me. Then I went back into the living room.

At one, she finally woke up. She came out of the bedroom with messy hair and smeared make up. My t-shirt reached past her knees and looked like a burlap sack on her. She sighed then rubbed her temple like she felt terrible.

"Morning, sweetheart." I poured her a glass of coffee then gave her some pain pills.

She eyed them both with squinted eyes, like the movement caused too much effort. "God, what happened last night...?"

I figured she wouldn't remember it. I ushered her to the table then sat her down. "Have some coffee and some breakfast." I made her a plate of toast and eggs then set it in front of her.

She pulled her hair back then wiped away the lines of mascara.

Even though she was a mess, she still looked beautiful to me. "You were drinking at a bar and some guy was harassing you. You called me to come get you and I put you in my bed and we went to sleep." I decided to leave out the good stuff. It would only embarrass her, and then I would have to explain why I got naked with her since I liked men.

She picked at her eggs but didn't eat them. She seemed lost in a cloud of confusion. Then suddenly, dramatically, her eyes widened to the size of acorns. "Oh my god…"

I sat next to her with a cup of coffee in my hand. "Remember now?"

"Vaguely…it comes and goes."

"Why were you that drunk?" I tried to keep the anger out of my voice. She wasn't my girlfriend so I had no right to get angry with her. It was a little early to show my true colors.

"I was out with my friends…" She ran her fingers through her hair and abandoned her food. "I had a lot of drinks because I was pissed off about Cameron…I don't really remember much else."

"Do you remember me getting you?"

"No," she said quietly. She kept moving her eggs around with her fork.

"You better eat that." I sounded more controlling than I meant to.

But she did as I asked.

"You do that often?"

"No," she said immediately. "Never."

"Just because someone hurt you doesn't give you the right to put yourself in dangerous situations. What you did was irresponsible and wrong. Do you have any idea how much you scared me? You can't do that to me ever again. This is never going to work if—" I realized what I was saying. "You need to take care of yourself. What would have happened if I hadn't made it in time? That guy was about to drag you out of there. And then—" I couldn't finish the sentence. It was too terrible to think about.

"It won't happen again." She didn't look at me like she was ashamed.

"Promise me." I needed to hear that otherwise I would never let her go out again.

"I promise."

"Look at me when you say it." My voice held my command.

She turned to me. "I promise."

That was what I needed. "Thank you."

Ophelia finished her breakfast in silence.

I just watched her.

"Thank you for getting me…"

"You're welcome."

There were a few crumbs left when she pushed the plate away. Her eyes were still squinted like the lights were on too bright, and her movements were sluggish like everything hurt.

"You can head back to bed if you want," I said.

"No, it's okay. I've been in your hair enough as it is."

My hand moved to hers. "You're always welcome here. I was just a little mad…because you scared me. That's all."

"Yeah?"

I held her gaze and nodded. "Yeah. Now go back to bed." I gave her a smile. "I'll have lunch ready when you wake up."

She smiled back at me then walked into my bedroom.

I watched her as she went, looking at those beautiful legs and remembering the way they felt when they were wrapped around me.

chapter 10

Ophelia

    That night was a disaster I never wanted to remember. I wish I had called Max to pick me up instead of Jett. Now I was embarrassed anytime I looked at him. I knew he was disappointed in me and how reckless my behavior was. That night could have ended a lot differently, and not in Jett's bed where I was safe.

    The week went by and I tried to move on and stop thinking about it. Jett and I went to the gym like normal but the relationship wasn't the same. I felt like I betrayed him in some way. I couldn't explain it or put my thumb on it, but the tension was there.

    I wish there was something I could do.

    Only time would make it easier. My friends checked in on me the following day, hoping I scored, but all I ended up doing was sleeping with a gay man, who happened to be my brother's boyfriend.

When did my life become this?

I sat at the kitchen table and flipped through a magazine.

Max came out of his bedroom then grabbed a beer from the refrigerator. "You seem down lately."

I assumed Jett hadn't told him what happened. If he had, Max would have mentioned it by now. "I'm just stressed out."

"Everything okay with Jett?"

"Yeah. We're just friends." I don't know why I blurted that out.

He nodded slowly. "Okay..."

I returned my attention back to the magazine. "How are you guys?"

"Good. No complaints."

"Good." But I knew I didn't mean it.

"Is the thing with Cameron still bothering you?"

I shrugged. "Not really. I'm over it."

"Then what's bothering you?"

"Nothing," I said defensively.

He held up his hands in surrender. "Okay...I'll back off."

I flipped the page so hard it tore.

Max went back into his bedroom and shut the door.

I poured myself a glass of wine and drank the whole thing in one gulp, hoping that would erase whatever was on my mind.

***

I tossed and turned that night in bed. My sheets wrapped around my body and hugged me. Sweat trickled down my body because of the heat of the room and my dreams. I kicked them off then felt cold so I pulled them back up. But I kept tossing and turning.

Then the dream came to me, hot like a poker right out of the fire.

Jett leaned back against his headboard and gripped my hips as he guided me up and down. Sweat was on his chest, and his eyes burned like simmering coals. He breathed hard while he rocked into me from below.

I massaged my tits while I sheathed him over and over. My hair flowed around my shoulders and bounced up and down every time I moved. His eyes burned into mine while he watched me.

"You're so gorgeous, sweetheart."

My nails dug into his shoulders harder as I rocked into him. His large hands gripped my ass and helped me move up and down his cock. "Jett..." I pressed my face to his and looked into his eyes.

"I'm so in love with you," he said through his labored breathing. "Deeply, madly, and truly."

His words lit the stick of dynamite and the explosion reached throughout my entire core. A scream came out of my throat as the delectable orgasm reached every nerve and fiber. "Oh god..."

His face moved into my chest and he sucked one nipple as he released inside me. "Sweetheart..."

I kept my arms tight around him as our sweaty bodies touched each other. My fingers moved into his hair as I treasured him against me. I never wanted to leave because the touch felt right. "I love you so much."

He looked into my eyes and cupped my face. "I love you."

The dream ended and I sat up in bed, covered in sweat and breathing hard. I pulled my hair out of my face then opened my eyes and looked around my bedroom. Jett wasn't there and I was alone. But I remembered every detail of the dream. The sex wasn't the most memorable thing. It was the gentleness of the way he kissed me, the way he made love to me while looking me in the eye, and the way his hand moved into my hair like he wanted to keep me forever. He said my intimate nickname, making me feel loved and cherished. It was a dream that I wished were real.

Then I realized it wasn't one of those dreams that meant nothing, like when you mowed your great aunt's lawn and she paid you in beetles. It hit me hard in that moment, and I knew exactly why the vision had come to me.

And I knew I had that dream many times—and not just tonight.

***

I was a terrible, terrible person.

Jett wasn't just my friend. He was my brother's boyfriend, a man I wasn't only attracted to, emotionally dependent on, but he was someone I saw as more than a friend.

I had feelings for him.
And he was my brother's boyfriend.
And he was gay.
What the hell was wrong with me?

I was in denial for the longest time. I kept the feelings deep down so I wouldn't realize them. But now I couldn't deny it anymore. Every time I saw Jett, butterflies rose up in my stomach. I couldn't stop smiling, especially when he gave me that cocky grin. I lived for the moments I shared with him. I didn't work out every day because I cared that much about being fit. I did it because I got to see him. I spent all my spare time with him because it was the only place I wanted to be.

He was the only person I wanted to be with.

My brother was one of my closest friends and I was crushing on his boyfriend.

I should be slapped hard across the face.

What was I going to do? I couldn't be around Jett anymore. These feelings would only get worse. Maybe if I avoided him long enough I would stop thinking about him all the time. Maybe the dreams would stop.

What other choice did I have?

***

Sweetheart, you want to hit the gym?

I stared at Jett's text message and read it several times. I thought about his beautiful face and gorgeous body. Shivers ran down my spine and I felt like I was floating on a cloud.

And that was why I couldn't see him.

Not today. I'll see you later. It was so hard to write that message. I was blowing him off and being vague about it. I would rather spend time with him but I was going home alone.

Everything okay?

I hated the fact he knew me so well. *Yeah, I'm just busy.*

Okay.

How long would I be able to keep this up?

***

I was watching TV on the couch when Max joined me. "How's the writing going?"

"Well," he said. "I think I'm onto something."

"Let me read it when you're done."

"If I ever find the courage," he said with a light laugh. "Jett is coming over, by the way."

I sat up quickly. "When?"

He eyed my quick movements suspiciously. "I don't know…in a few minutes."

I had to get out of there before Jett arrived. I jumped off the couch then pulled a sweatshirt over my head. After I grabbed a magazine and a book, I shouldered my purse then headed for the door.

"What are you doing?" Max asked.

"I just remembered I have to go to he office."

"You've never had to go to the office at night before…"

"Well, things change." I walked out. "Bye." I shut the door quickly then practically ran down the stairs so I could get out of the building before Jett entered. If we crossed paths, it would be too awkward.

I crossed the street and moved passed people, grateful that I avoided running into him. When I arrived at my office, I shut the door then turned on my lamp. Then I read a magazine at my desk and waited for the night to pass.

***

I managed to avoid Jett for almost two entire weeks. Whenever he came over, I left the apartment. Whenever Jett asked me to do something, I made an excuse not to see him. Even though I was limiting my contact with him the distance didn't stop the feelings. They were as strong as ever.

When I got off work that day, I walked out and headed the opposite way of the gym. I told Jett I sprained my ankle and I shouldn't work out anymore. That got him off my back for a while.

"Hey, sweetheart." His voice wasn't full of warmth like it usually was. Actually, it was ice-cold.

I stopped and turned to him, seeing him lean against the building. He wore dark jeans and a deep green t-shirt. I hated the fact he looked hotter than ever before.

His hair was slightly messy but it looked good on him. His gorgeous body invited me to him and I somehow resisted.

He approached me with his hands in his pockets. "What's the deal?"

I kept a straight face. "Deal? What deal?"

"Why are you avoiding me?" He searched my eyes, looking for a lie.

"I'm not." I stepped away. "I'm in a hurry and I should get going." I was already falling under his spell.

He grabbed me by the wrist and yanked me toward him. "You think I'm stupid?" He got in my face, the anger brewing in his eyes.

"No, I just—"

"Don't lie to me. Why are you avoiding me?"

"I just…I'm busy." I couldn't think of anything else to say.

"You're busy?" he asked incredulously. *"You're busy?"*

"Why are you spending so much time with me anyway?" I asked. "You should be spending it with Max."

"Whoa…what?" He stepped back like he was stung. "What the hell is that supposed to mean?"

"You spend too much time with me. The only person you should make that much effort with is Max." I was on the offensive, trying to make him angry enough to leave me alone.

"How about you let me worry about my relationship with Max? And I can have other friends."

"Just leave me alone, okay?" I tried to walk away.

"No." He snatched me again. "Is this about the night at the bar?"

"No."

"Are you sure?" He searched my face again.

What could have happened that night that would make me stop talking to him? "Yes. I just need space."

"Space from what?" he snapped. "Last time I checked, we were good friends that spend a lot of time together. Now you drop me quicker than a hat. What's that about?"

Why wouldn't he just back off? "I have other friends, Jett. I have other responsibilities and obligations."

"Oh really?" he said coldly. "Like the two friends that ditched you at that bar? If I remember correctly, I was the one you called to help you. I was the first person you thought of. You trusted me to save you. And now you're just dumping me?"

"I'm not dumping you. I just don't want to see you every single day."

"Why not?" he asked. "We've been doing it for the past four months. What's changed?"

This was getting too hard. I tried not to let the tears build up. I loved Jett and I hated hurting him. "Just give me space." I didn't know what else to say. There was no excuse I could make other than the truth. Nothing would make sense. "Leave me alone."

Jett's eyes fell with sadness and he looked devastated. The aggression left his voice. "I'm sorry…for whatever it is I did."

God, I was a terrible person.

He stepped back, a resigned look on his face. "I guess I'll give you some space." He turned away and walked up the street, his shoulders sagging under an invisible weight.

***

I'd never felt worse.

I hit rock bottom.

Jett and I hadn't spoken in weeks. He didn't reach out to me again, and I didn't talk to him.

I felt like I lost a piece of my soul.

He was my best friend, not just the man I loved, and not having him was like living without air and water. He was always on my mind, and whenever I wasn't distracted by something, he was in my thoughts.

How did I fall in love with a gay man?

A gay man who was dating my brother?

I deserved to feel this pain. This wouldn't have happened if I hadn't been stupid. Only someone truly messed up in the head would be in this situation. First, I stayed with a man who clearly didn't love me, and then I loved a man who would never love me back.

I had some serious issues.

Max knocked on my bedroom door while I lay in bed, feeling sorry for myself. "Ophelia?"

"Hmm?"

"Can we talk?"

"About?" I didn't get up to answer the door.

"Can I open the door?"

I shrugged even though he couldn't see me.

"As much as I love talking to you through a door, it's getting old."

I sighed then sat up. "Come in."

Max opened the door then sat at the edge of my bed. He regarded me for a moment, pity in his eyes. "What happened with you and Jett?"

Did Jett say something to him? "Nothing..."

"Well, he told me you didn't want to see him anymore, and you're completely miserable every time I see you. So something did happen."

I wouldn't be able to hide this forever, not from my brother. I was afraid to tell him because I was scared of his reaction. *Would he hate me? Would he push me away just like he did to our parents? Would we ever come back from this?*

"Talk to me." He rested his arms on his thighs.

It was easier just to tell the truth. He would tell Jett, and then everything would make sense. Jett would stay away from me, and my brother would probably move out. I'd be able to get over him.

"Come on, sis. It's me."

I took a deep breath. "You're going to hate me..."

"Never."

"Don't say that too soon," I said sadly.

He scooted closer to me. "I could never hate you. My parents have deserted me and I still don't hate them."

My actions made me worse.

"Try me, Ophelia."

"Okay…here it goes."

He patiently waited for me to speak.

"I don't know how or when it happened…but it did. Jett and I spent a lot of time together. We went to the gym together, out to dinner, and I even slept at his place countless times. And while I know he's gay and he loves you…somehow…I fell in love with him." The truth was out and I slightly felt better. Hoarding the secret was killing me and now some of the weight was off my shoulders. "I'm so sorry. I never pursued him or told him how I felt. I would never do that to you…but having feelings for him is still unforgiveable." I crossed my arms over my chest and stared at the ground.

Max didn't look at me. He massaged his knuckles and released a deep sigh.

"I'm so sorry…" I couldn't lose my brother. I loved him so much.

"That's why you don't want to see him anymore?"

"I can't get over him if he's still in my life."

He released another sigh.

"I told you it was bad."

"Ophelia, it's okay. Don't beat yourself up over it."

"How could I not?" I snapped. "If you were my sister, everyone would tell you to disown me. I practically betrayed you."

"But you didn't," he said.

"Yes, I did. Jett is yours and I've been thinking about him in ways I'm not entitled to…"

"Ophelia, I'm not mad," he said calmly.

"How can that be possible?"

He watched his knuckles as he massaged them again. "Because I'm not."

I shook my head. "If the situation were reversed, I wouldn't sweep it under the rug."

"Maybe because the situation isn't what it seems…"

"Meaning?"

He stood up then put his hands in his pockets. "I need to talk to Jett. We'll continue this conversation later."

"You need to talk to him right this second?" I asked incredulously. "Aren't you going to yell at me? Disown me?"

"No," he said simply.

"You're going to tell Jett what I said?"

He nodded.

At least it would be easier this way. I could never tell him I loved him to his face. He would avoid me and not feel bad about it. "I hope he doesn't hate me."

"I have a strong feeling he won't." He walked out then shut the door.

I lay back down and hugged a pillow to my chest. I stared at the ceiling and imagined how the conversation would go. Jett would be surprised, even shocked, and then they would have to keep their relationship away from me. Maybe one day I would be over it and we could all be in the same room together.
But it would never be the same.

Dangerous Stranger

Chapter 11

Jett

A pain thudded deep in my chest and I felt sicker than I ever had on my worst day on earth. My heart didn't pump blood properly because it was broken. It simply didn't work anymore. Every muscle in my body lost its ability to move. All I wanted to do was lie in bed and wonder what I did to push Ophelia away.

She wanted nothing to do with me.

She told me she needed space, that she was busy and had other friends to hang out with. She didn't have time for me.

She didn't want to make time for me.

Everything was fine one day, and then the next she was gone. We spent every day together, and then she didn't want to see me anymore. I picked her up from the bar then took her home. We made out naked on my bed then slept together. Then everything was different from that point onward.

I wondered if she remembered what happened between us. Maybe that triggered our break up. What if she realized what happened between us, that we rubbed our naked bodies together and almost made love. But when I asked her, she didn't mention it.

Why would she hide it?

But what else could have happened?

It was killing me.

I knew Ophelia was a big part of my life but I didn't realize how big until she was gone. She was the only woman in my life, the person I lived for. I found myself walking past her office and lunchtime in the hope of seeing her. I went to Max's so I could run into her. But none of those ploys ever worked.

And now I was drowning.

I'd never had a relationship before so I never had a break up either.

And man, they sucked.

I felt like I was getting divorced. That's how much it hurt. The guys were my best friends, but Ophelia had a special place in my heart. I told her everything. Being without her was like going back to my former life. I was never sad before, but after I had a taste of paradise I realized my previous life was just a desert.

I found myself drinking at bars more often. The time I would normally spend with Ophelia was spent drowning in alcohol. I would sit at the bar until it closed at some unearthly hour. Then the barman would kick me out. When I went home, I just drank more.

I was pathetic.

***

I was lying on the couch throwing a football in the air when there was a knock on the door.

"Come in." I couldn't care less who it was. If it was the President of the United States, hopefully he liked football.

The door opened and footsteps were heard.

I kept tossing the ball in the air. "Welcome, stranger."

"It's me." Max's voice came to my ear.

I talked to him a few days ago about Ophelia. I asked if he knew anything about her estrangement. He said he didn't have a clue. I thought there might be a guy in her life but he said she hadn't brought anyone back to the apartment.

Thank god.

"What can I do for you?" I asked as I kept tossing the ball into the air. "A family dinner, perhaps?"

He walked to the couch then grabbed the football out of the air. "We need to talk."

"About?"

"Ophelia."

That caught my attention so I sat up. "What about her? Is she okay?"

"No, she's not okay." He took the seat beside me. "Not at all."

"What's going on?"

He rubbed the back of his neck. "I changed my mind about what I said."

I didn't know what he meant.

"You have my permission to tell her the truth." He tossed the ball at me.

I caught it without looking. "What…?"

"I found out the reason why she's avoiding you."

My shoulders straightened and my heart stopped beating for three seconds.

"She told me she's in love with you." He looked me in the eye as he said it.

My heart started beating again, and this time, it slammed hard in my chest. My entire body kicked into overdrive. I came alive. The depression that consumed me for weeks seemed to evaporate. I slowly rose to my feet, feeling my arms shake. "Say that again."

He smirked. "She's in love with you."

"So…she actually said that?"

He nodded. "Word for word."

I started to pace the living room. I knocked over a lamp as I moved and I didn't even notice. "So, she's been avoiding me because she has feelings for me."

He nodded. "She feels terrible because she thinks you're my boyfriend. And she thinks you're gay."

Now a smile spread across my lips. "Yes! I knew there was something between us. I knew it!" I turned my attention back to him. "What did you tell her?"

"Nothing. She needs to hear the truth from you, not me."

I grabbed my wallet and keys. "I'll tell her right now."

"Whoa, hold on." He stood up and raised his hand. "You need to go about this carefully."

"Why?" I demanded. "I love her. I'll tell her that. Problem solved."

"And you think she's just going to say it back and everything will be fine?" he asked incredulously.

What am I missing? "Why wouldn't it be okay?"

He rubbed his temple. "You've been gay to her for four months. You think she's going to appreciate the fact it was all a lie?"

"She knew on some deep level. The way we were together…she knew."

"I really don't think she did, man."

"Look, I know her in a way you don't."

"I'm sure you do," he said. "But I know I'm right about this. She doesn't know anything about you—just the lies you've projected. You think that's not going to hurt her?"

"I'll explain to her that I couldn't tell her the truth. I didn't lie because I wanted to."

He shrugged his shoulders. "I don't know how she'll react exactly, but it's not going to be in the fairytale way you're imagining."

"All that matters is we love each other. We'll figure it out."

"I hope you're right," he said quietly.

Now he implanted a seed of doubt into my mind. What if she didn't love me with open arms? What if she pushed me away? "Then what do you think I should do?"

"You only have one option, right? You have to tell her the truth. I just don't want you to get your hopes up."

"Maybe you're right," I admitted. "Maybe things won't work out the way I want. But they will work out. She and I will get through it. She might be hurt at first but she'll stick it out."

"Of all the men I've met, you deserve her the most. So I hope you get her."

"I will get her." I headed to the door. "Lock up when you leave."

"I got nowhere to go so I'll stick around until you come home."

"I have a feeling I'll won't be back until morning."

***

I knocked on her door and waited for an answer. When the door didn't open, I knocked again. If she were avoiding me on purpose she wouldn't get away with it. She was going to face me.

"Ophelia! Answer the door." I rocked my fist against the wood.

Finally, she cracked the door open. Through the small crack, I could see she was wearing yoga pants and a t-shirt. Her hair was pulled up in a messy bun. Her face was free of make up. "Max isn't here." She started to close the door again.

I stuck my foot in the crack so the door wouldn't close. "I'm here to talk to you."

She nervously tucked a strand of hair behind her ear. "Well, I'm busy."

I barged inside then slammed the door behind me.

She backed up quickly, looking at me in a way she never had before. Fear was in her eyes. She was no longer comfortable around me. Shame was registered on her face. The embarrassment was evident too.

Now that I was there, I didn't know what to say. The moment had come. I could tell her exactly how I felt, that she was the one woman I wanted in my bed every night. I cared about her more than I'd ever cared about another person. She was my life. What words could I say to explain that? "I talked to Max."

She nodded slightly. "Oh…"

"And he told me what you said—about me."

She averted her gaze and stared at the floor. "I…I'm so sorry. The last thing I want to do is interfere in your relationship. My feelings are harmless, I swear." Her voice shook at the end.

I closed the gap between us and placed my forehead against hers. "I feel the same way, Ophelia. I've felt that way for a long time—since the moment we met."

She looked up at me, and confusion came into her eyes. Her eyes darted back and forth as she searched my face. Her lips moved slightly, making a surprised look. "What…?"

"Ophelia, I love you. I've loved you for a long time."

She still didn't understand. "But…how is that possible?"

"It's a long story but…I'm not gay. I've never been gay. I will never be gay."

Wordlessly, she questioned me.

"I'm a professional escort. Your brother paid me to pretend to be his boyfriend to make a good first impression with his parents—and you. I did as he asked, but the second I met you I couldn't stay away. I wanted to get warm from your fire.

"I asked Max if I could tell you the truth a month ago. But he said I couldn't. Spending every day with you has never been friendly on my part. To me, you are everything. To me, you mean the world. I've wanted you for so long and it was torture not having you. When you told Max how you felt, he realized he couldn't keep us apart just for his own gain. So, now I'm telling you the truth, that I'm madly in love with you." I looked into her eyes and watched her reaction. There wasn't much to work with. Her eyes narrowed but she didn't speak. I had no idea what she was thinking. I waited for her to say something, to tell me how relieved she was we could finally be together.

But she remained silent.

I gripped her hips and leaned in. I kissed her on the mouth and tasted her lips. I'd already kissed her before so I knew exactly how it felt but it still caught me by surprise. I squeezed her to my body and breathed into her mouth, loving every second of it.

She kissed me back, slowly and not with as much enthusiasm as before. Her lips didn't possess as much life, and not nearly as much passion. Then she broke apart altogether. "I'm sorry…it's just a lot to take in."

I knew I dropped a lot on her. "I understand." I didn't kiss her but I kept my hands on her.

"You've been straight this entire time?"

"And madly in love with you." That was the important part.

"So, when we were in the changing room together…you were straight?"

I watched her change and that was probably a bad idea. "Well…yeah."

"And you saw me naked…" She looked mortified.

"You had your underwear on." That was a stupid thing to say.

Her cheeks blushed. "And when I slept with you…you were straight."

"Yeah…"

"All this time, you've been straight."

Was it that hard to understand?

"So…nothing about you is true."

"No, that's where you're wrong. Everything else about me is true."

"But you aren't a pharmaceutical inventor. You're an escort."

"Well, that's the only thing," I said.

She shook her head. "I just…feel like I don't know you anymore."

"Don't say that. You do know me. And we can get to know each other again if that's what you want. I'm more than patient."

"So, you've never been gay?"

"I've always been straight." I already said this. Our reunion was not going the way I wanted—at all.

"Have you ever had a serious girlfriend before? Have you ever been married? I don't know any of that."

"The answer to both questions is no."

She nodded but didn't seem satisfied with that response.

"Sweetheart, nothing is different. Now we can have what we want."

"Cameron…" She paused while she gathered her thoughts. "All that stuff that happened with him, him getting sick, him spilling the wine, and you catching him cheating on me…that was all you."

I sighed. "I may have tailed him to see what he was up to. But it wasn't to break you up so I could have you. It was to keep you away from him because he's a dog that doesn't deserve you."

"When you asked me not to sleep with him—"

"I knew he was cheating on you. I just didn't have the proof yet."

She stepped back and crossed her arms over her chest. "I feel like my world is completely turned upside down. What I thought I knew was true is just a lie. I don't know what to make of it."

I cupped her face and forced her to look at me. "Everything between us was real. That is the only thing that matters anyway." I kissed the corner of her mouth then pulled away. "When I kissed your tears away, that was real. When I slept with you and ran my fingers through your hair that was real. When I beat the shit out of Cameron three times to defend you that was real. What I feel for you is true. Ophelia, that's all that matters. Let's take it slow and you can see that."

"I don't know." She took another step back.

"Don't shut me out," I said immediately.

"Cameron lied to me. Our whole relationship was a lie. And…that really hurt. And now this feels the same way."

"Don't you dare compare me to him." My words came out as a growl. "Ever. I actually care about you. I actually love you. It's not the same thing."

Dangerous Stranger

"It was still all a lie, even if it was under a different context."

I gripped her arm and dragged her back to me. "No, it's not. I was doing my job and I couldn't throw Max under the bus. Don't be like this, Ophelia."

"Do you really not understand my point of view?" Her voice grew stronger, full of anger. "I've been hating myself for weeks for betraying Max. I didn't understand how I could fall for a gay man. It made me question myself entirely. But to know you were straight the whole time...I feel like a fool."

"You aren't a fool," I said gently. "I was hitting on you left and right. I wanted you to fall for me so when my assignment ended I could have you."

"So you messed with me on purpose?"

"No, I didn't *mess* with you. I may have amazing skills but I can't make someone fall in love with me."

"I changed in front of you..." Her cheeks reddened to tomatoes.

"And it was a beautiful sight." I didn't see the point in being ashamed. "I already stared at your ass whether you were wearing anything or not."

The anger flashed in her eyes. "You shouldn't have gone in the changing room with me."

"I know," I admitted. "But fuck, I'm only human. Cut me some slack."

"This is just too weird. I feel like you're a different person."

Why was this happening? Why did Max have to be right? "Ophelia, I'm not asking you to be mine immediately. We can take this slow. Let me take you on a date and you can get to know me—the real me. You'll see that I'm exactly the same person."

"I don't know…"

"I do," I said firmly. "Give me a chance. Don't just throw me away. We both know we're perfect together."

"How could I possibly know that?" she demanded. "When I don't know you and I don't trust you?" She stared me in the eye as her words lingered in the air. The accusation and anger floated like a cloud.

Now I was getting mad. "That night I picked you up from that bar, I took you to my place. The second I put you on my bed you started kissing me. And I don't mean something gentle and innocent. Your tongue was down my throat instantly."

Her eyes widened at my words. She seemed genuinely surprised so she must not remember.

"Then you took off your dress and your thong then you ripped off my clothes. We made out together, totally naked on my bed, and you begged me to make love to you. Do you not remember it?"

She shook her head and looked away.

"I've never been more attracted to a woman in my life and I wanted you—so bad. You were underneath me with your legs around my waist. I could have taken you and you wouldn't have even remembered it. But I didn't. I put your clothes back on and made you go to sleep. Maybe I'm not perfect and I didn't handle this situation in the best way, but I'm not a terrible guy. I looked at your ass when I shouldn't but I didn't fuck you when you were wasted. So, that's the kind of guy I am. And that's all you need to know."

My words didn't seem to have a positive effect. If anything, she seemed embarrassed. She stepped away from me and headed to her room. Without looking back at me or speaking, she closed the door and locked it.

Fuck, why was this happening to me?

***

Ophelia refused to speak to me or talk to me. Every time I called she didn't answer. Every time I went to her apartment, she didn't answer. Max wasn't much help. Every time I spoke to him, he shrugged and gave me that look that said, "I told you so."

How did I fix this?

How did I get her back?

Maybe she just needed time. It would be difficult to believe one thing about a person you considered to be your best friend and then to be told it was a complete lie. I tried to be sympathetic to her position but it was difficult. Why couldn't I just hold her while she acclimated to the change? I hated being shut out.

Not having Ophelia in my life was driving me crazy. Whenever I was at the gym, it didn't feel the same without her. When I slept in my bed, I wished she were lying beside me. There were times when I saw something funny and wanted to tell her about it but I couldn't.

I missed her.

Did I really find the girl of my dreams just to lose her?

I wouldn't take this defeat lying down. Maybe she didn't know if she could trust me but I could convince her otherwise. I'd never given up on anything in my life. It would be stupid to give up on the one thing that actually mattered.

***

I knew what time she got off work so I headed to her office. I didn't want to corner her on the street and scare her. At least this way she knew I was coming. And she knew she couldn't get away.

Her secretary spotted me then spoke over the intercom. "Jett is here to see you."

I didn't need to remind her who I was. She remembered me. "Thanks."

Ophelia's voice came over the intercom. "Tell him I'm very busy."

Burn. "I have a surprise for her." I smiled at her assistant, trying to charm her.

"Go on in." She batted her eyelashes at me then returned to work.

I walked into her office then shut the door behind me.

Ophelia released a loud sigh, clearly wanting me to hear. "I'm very busy, Jett."

"You get off work in…" I looked at my watch. "One minute. I doubt you're that busy."

She pulled her hair over on shoulder, what she usually did when she was flustered. "Coming to my office is inappropriate."

"Well, we both know I've never been appropriate." I approached her desk and leaned over it. "Let's get coffee after work."

"No."

I leaned further until our lips were almost touching. "Yes."

Her breath fell on my skin and she glanced at my lips.

She still wanted me. "I'm not going to stop until I get a few minutes of your time. I suggest you cooperate."

"Okay, *Cameron*."

I let the burn wash over me. "Stop comparing me to him. You don't want to see me mad."

"I've seen you mad before."

"No, you haven't." I held her gaze for a moment before I dropped it. "Let's finish up and let's go."

She gave me a venomous glare before she stacked up her papers and put her computer to sleep. Then she grabbed her purse and flipped her hair over one shoulder.

I stared at her as she came around her desk. She wore a black dress with a gray cardigan. Heels were on her feet. She looked sexy, like always. I opened the door for her, showing her I was the same man I used to be.

She glanced at the gesture then walked out.

We walked out of the building and to the sidewalk in silence. She seemed determined to remain quiet. I was saving my ammunition for the coffee shop. When she was sitting across from me and looking at me, there was nowhere for her to go.

We reached a Starbucks and I opened the door for her. "This place sounds as good as any."

She walked inside then stood in line.

"What are you getting?"

"I can get it," she said quickly.

Why was she being so stubborn? "I insist."

"It's fine."

"I suggest you stop being a brat before I make you."

She met my look without flinching.

Then I gripped her neck and pressed a hard kiss to her lips.

She flinched at the touch but didn't push me off or try to stop me.

I pulled away. "Now tell me what the fuck you want."

"Iced black tea," she said like a robot.

"Now take a seat and I'll be there in a second." I try to keep my voice low so I wouldn't attract the attention of other people in line.

She did as I asked.

After I got our drinks, I sat in the seat across from her.

Polite as always, she put the straw in her drink and said, "Thank you."

"You're welcome, sweetheart." I tried to be gentle since I was pretty harsh on her a second ago.

She sipped her drink then stared at me, clearly not willing to speak first.

"I went to NYU for college. I majored in business. When I graduated, I had a ton of student loans. Rhett came up with the idea of us escorting people in desperate need of dates. It was good and easy money but soon it started to snowball. We were quickly making more money doing that than anything else we could possibly do. So, it just stuck."

She nodded her head slightly in understanding. "And you sleep with people?"

She thought I did? No wonder why she was so distant with me. "No, absolutely not. We just do handholding and waist touching. That's it. We have strict rules about that kind of stuff."

She breathed a noticeable sigh of relief. "And when you slept in Max's room…"

"I slept on an air mattress on the floor—alone."

"I see…"

Hopefully that would make her warm up to me. Who wanted to date a prostitute? "My job isn't just being somebody's date. There's more to it than that. I make a lot of lifelong friends. Max is a good example of that. I really like him as a person and I'm glad I could help him in whatever way I could. I'm just sad it didn't work out the way he wanted."

She stared at me with unreadable eyes. "If you've never had a girlfriend before, does that mean you sleep around?"

I knew this question would come up. "Yeah." I wasn't going to hide it or lie.

Disappointment filled her eyes. "I'm not that kind of girl, Jett."

"I know. Why do you think I'm in love with you?"

She rolled her eyes. "So typical. You sleep with all of Manhattan but will only settle down for a girl with a low number. I hate sexist pigs like you. So, if I slept around I wouldn't be good enough for you?"

This was backfiring. "That's not what I'm saying at all. I'm just attracted to the fact that you respect yourself. That's all. You don't need male attention like most girls. It has nothing to do with the number of guys you slept with. You're the most gorgeous woman I've seen, and that's saying something sense I live in Manhattan, and you're totally blind to it. Now that's sexy as hell."

She crossed her arms over her chest, pushing her breasts up without realizing it.

I did my very best not to look.

"So, for the past four months you've been sleeping with random women?" Disdain was in her voice.

"I haven't slept with anyone since the day I met you." That was the truth. She was the only woman I had in my bed. "I got offers, like usual. But I didn't want that. I want you." Sincerity shined in my eyes. "I've never wanted to be in a relationship because they seem boring and repetitive. You can only have sex with the same person so many times before you're bored out of your mind. But my friends have been settling down and I've never seen them happier. Then when I met you…it all made sense."

"You haven't slept with me. I may be boring and repetitive." Sarcasm leaked in her voice.

"I've fooled around with you. Believe me, it wasn't boring."

She looked away, unable to stand the heat in my eyes.

I leaned over the table. "What else do you want to know about me?"

"You have an STD?" It was a jab, not a serious question.

"No. I get checked often." I didn't rise to the insult.

She kept her arms across her chest.

"You're being really stupid right now." The words came out without thinking.

"Excuse me?"

"We love each other. I fell in love with you the moment I laid eyes on you. You fell in love with me…I'm not sure when. And that's all that matters. I know it's under unusual circumstances but the situation doesn't change who we are. You and I connected on a deep level. It was just there the second we met."

"But I was open with you because I thought you were gay," she hissed. "I never would have been so forward or honest if you were just some guy trying to sleep with me. So, the circumstance does make a difference."

"I just wanted to sleep with you in the beginning but that quickly changed. I want to be with you for many reasons, and sex is the last one on the list. And it's a good thing you thought I was gay. We wouldn't have had this budding friendship without it. You may not have fallen in love with me without it."

"It was still deceitful."

Was she never going to come around? Was this the end? She ended the relationship before it began just because I wasn't honest about my sexual orientation? "We're already in a relationship, Ophelia. It may not have been official and it may not have been traditional but we were. We spent all our time together, and when the times got tough, you turned to me for help. You could have called anyone else but you called me—because you trust me."

"I *trusted* you." She didn't look at me.

Why was she being so difficult about this? "You're really prepared to let me go over this?" Disbelief was in my voice. "You're ready to throw away everything we had just because you thought I was gay?"

"It's more complicated than that and you know it."

"You're still willing to lose the man you love over it?" I asked incredulously. "That's the bottom line."

She turned back to me. "I don't know what happened to the man I love. But he isn't you."

Those words crashed and burned in my chest. Nothing had ever hurt me so much. I lost my purpose in life. She ripped out my heart then shoved it into her tea, letting it freeze along with the ice cubes. She tossed me aside because she no longer wanted me. I was nothing to her, just a random person on the street.

I felt like shit.

Worse than shit.

My hands started to shake on the table so I pulled them into my lap so she couldn't see them. To say I was devastated was an understatement. If I'd known this was how she was going to react I wouldn't have told her the truth at all. I would have continued to be her gay friend because at least she was in my life that way.

Now she was gone.

I couldn't think of anything to say. I rose to a stand and left my untouched coffee on the table. When I looked at her, those green eyes shined back at me. There was anger and hurt in the look. I opened my mouth to speak but nothing came out. I'd officially given up. This wasn't going to go anywhere. I was pedaling a canoe upstream. I could make it if only I had another person to paddle. But I didn't. I stepped away from the table and walked out of the coffee shop. I turned my back on her and walked away, feeling weaker with every step I took.

I lost her and I would never have her again.

I'd given up.

chapter 12

Ophelia

I'd never forget the devastated look in Jett's eyes. He looked like the ground had been pulled out from directly underneath him. When he walked away, his shoulders weren't broad like they once were. They sagged under the weight of his grief. But I sat there and watched him go. I didn't stop him.

The weeks passed without anything eventful coming to pass. Time seemed to move like a blur. All I remembered doing was going to work then coming home. I'd been eating a lot of frozen waffles because I didn't have the motivation to go to the grocery store.

Jett didn't call me.
I didn't call him.
I guess we were through.

He came to me in my dreams, and while they were beautiful and passionate, I wished they would stop. It was just torture. I couldn't have him so the experiences were painful.

I couldn't get over all the lies he told me. The entire relationship was based on fiction. I was so embarrassed for being so open with him. He was straight the entire time and I felt like he played me. There were moments when I questioned his orientation but I didn't dwell on it long because I assumed he wouldn't lie to me.

I was wrong about that.

There were times when I missed him so much that I didn't care. But then the feeling of betrayal came back and I didn't want to look at him ever again. Fortunately, he never came to the apartment so I didn't have to worry about it. He didn't contact me, and it didn't seem like he contacted Max either.

I was sitting on the couch when Max grabbed his wallet and keys from the table. He was dressed in jeans and a black blazer. "You look nice."

"Jerome and I are going out." He put his watch on his wrist then clasped it.

Jerome was his real boyfriend, who I hadn't met. "Have fun."

He approached the couch while he adjusted his watch. "So, you and Jett are done for good?"

Why was he asking me that now? "Yeah."

"Good," he said with a nod.

Good? "Why is that good?"

"Well…" He shrugged in guilt. "I'm actually going on a double date with him tonight. He met some girl at a bar. I didn't get all the details."

My heart fell into my stomach. "He's…dating?" We hadn't spoken in two weeks but that felt sudden.

"Apparently," he said with a shrug. "We're going to that new bar and club The Flamingo. It should be fun." He adjusted his jacket and checked the sleeves.

I felt sick.

"You're cool with it, right?" he asked as he looked me in the eye. "Because I won't go if it makes you uncomfortable…"

"No, it's fine," I said with a voice that didn't sound like my own.

"Are you sure?" he asked.

"Yeah." My voice cracked slightly.

"Alright," he said. "I'm sleeping at Jerome's so don't expect me until sometime tomorrow."

"Okay." My fingers tingled with weakness.

"See ya." He walked out and locked the door behind him.

I turned off the TV and just sat there in silence. My eyes started to burn with impending tears. I blinked quickly to keep them back. Why the hell am I crying? I told Jett it would never work. I let him walk out of the coffee shop with that hollow look in his eyes. What did I expect him to do? Mourn me forever?

***

Unable to believe what I was doing, I stood outside The Flamingo. I tossed my pajamas and wore the black dress Jett picked out when we went shopping. It was backless and tight, and I wore heels that made me look five inches taller. Guys passed me on the sidewalk, and when they whistled I knew the outfit was a good choice.

What the hell was I doing?

Was I going to storm in there and interrupt his date? How petty was that? I didn't want him but he couldn't be with someone else? Every time I thought about him sleeping with someone it made me want to crawl into a ball under my bed and die like a skunk.

I didn't get in line because I still wasn't sure what I was doing. What did I expect to accomplish by walking in there? Did I really think Jett would forget about his date and take me back now that my head was on straight? That would never happen. I should just go. I missed my chance.

"Damn, girl. You look fine." The bouncer eyed me up and down. "Get in here." He unhooked the rope to let me pass then nodded me inside.

Without thinking, I walked inside. His attention stole my focus, and before I knew it, I was in the crowded club passing through people. A few guys turned in my direction but I kept going and tried to ignore them.

Finding Jett and Max in this crowded place would be difficult. They could be on the dance floor or in one of the booths. Or they could be at the bar. It would be a long search.

Dangerous Stranger

I started off at the bar but didn't see them. Then I moved toward the tables, discreetly glancing in the dark booths. I recognized my brother before Jett. His dark blazer and dark hair made him stand out.

Jett sat on the other side of the booth and was listening to something Max was saying. But he was alone. There was no girl beside him. Perhaps she was in the bathroom.

What the hell was I doing? I looked like a stalker right now.

My feet carried me closer to them and I watched their interaction. Max was sitting beside a dark skinned man that looked at least six foot four. His hand was on his thigh. I assumed that was Jerome.

Jett's eyes left Max and turned on me. When he saw me, he didn't react. He just stared at me.

I stared back, suddenly feeling self-conscious in my tight dress and ridiculous heels. I stayed rooted to the spot, feeling my knees ache from standing still for so long.

Jett leaned back in his chair and regarded me with unreadable eyes.

I couldn't tell if he hated me or not. It was a look I'd never seen before.

Jett left the booth then walked toward me. He wore the dark jeans I loved to see him wear. They hung low on his hips and hinted at his defined body. His broad chest was highlighted in a gray t-shirt. When I remembered him shirtless, I realized everything I was missing. He stopped when he was in front of me then stared me down.

I stared back.

"What brings you here?" His voice was void of emotion.

"Uh..." I stuttered like a loser. "I'm just here with some friends."

"Where are they?"

"Around," I said with a shrug.

He nodded his head slowly. "Are you really here with friends?" He knew the real answer.

"No..."

"Then why are you here?" He put his hands in his pockets while he stared me down.

"Honestly, I don't know."

He seemed disappointed with that response. "I guess I'll give you some time to figure it out." He turned to walk back to the booth.

"Wait." I grabbed his arm and pulled him back.

He looked at me again. "What?"

"Max told me you were on a date..." I swallowed the lump in my throat.

"What if I am?" he snapped. "You don't want me, right?"

"I...I never said that."

"Yes you did," he barked. "Not in those exact words but you did. Now, if you'll excuse me, I'm on a date with a woman who does want me. And she'll be fucking my brains out tonight." He turned away again.

The idea of him being with another woman made me want to vomit all over my shoes. Tears burned in my eyes. "Wait." I grabbed him again and pulled him back. "I'm sorry, okay?"

"Sorry for what?" His eyes held no mercy.

"For pushing you away."

"Well, I forgive you. Now let me go."

"I don't want to let you go…" I blinked quickly so the tears wouldn't fall.

He watched me passively. "What are you saying?"

"That I was being stupid and…I'd really like another chance if you're willing. I really don't want you to go home with some other girl tonight—as selfish as that sounds." I took a deep breath so the tears wouldn't fall.

Finally, the anger in his eyes evaporated. That cocky smile I'd fallen in love with stretched across his face. "I'm too good to share, huh?"

He pulled a one eighty and I didn't know what to make of it.

"You're just as greedy as I am." His hands moved to my hips. "I don't like to share either."

"What…?"

"I'm on a date but not with who you think."

I was still confused.

"You're my date—and you're late." He pulled me to his chest and brushed his lips past mine.

"There's no one else...?" Hope fluttered in my heart.

"Come on, sweetheart. There will never be anyone else." He wrapped his arms around me and pulled me closer. He looked down into my face with a slight grin on his lips.

"So, you just had Max say that so I would come down here?"

"Don't get mad about it," he said quickly. "Yes, I lied and manipulated you. But that was the only thing that would get through that thick skull of yours." He playfully rapped his knuckles against my head. "Now, will you sit down with me and be my date for the evening?"

All the pain went away when I realized there was no one else. It took me a long time to get here but I was grateful I was there now. Jett was mine and he'd always been mine. "Can we stay for like an hour?"

"Why?"

"Because I really want to head to your place as soon as possible."

His grin widened and his eyes sparkled with delight. "Then let's get this stupid date over with." He pulled me to the table and scooted me into the booth.

"You're late," Max said as he glanced at his watch.

Jett put his arm around my shoulders. "As long as she's here, she's on time."

***

Once we crossed the threshold of his apartment, he was all over me. "You really shouldn't have worn that dress." He turned me around and pressed my stomach against the kitchen island. Then he sent warm kisses down my back.

"Why? I love it when you touch me."

He grabbed my ass and released a moan as he kissed the back of my neck. "Like this?"

"Uh-huh."

He kneeled and lifted up my dress, kissing my legs all the way to my ass. "And how about like this?"

"Yeah…"

He moved back to his feet then guided me from the kitchen toward his bedroom. His hands moved everywhere and his lips were on my neck like a blood-sucking mosquito.

When we were in his bedroom, he guided me to the bed then leaned over me. "You know, we don't have to do this now." Judging the look in his eyes he didn't want to wait—for anything. "There's no rush."

"We've been dating for four months. We've waited long enough."

His eyes smiled. "You have a point." He kissed my chest as he slowly removed my dress. He pulled it down my body and kissed my navel piercing as he did it. When the dress was off he left my heels on then moved to my thong. He kissed my inner thighs and pulled one leg over his shoulder.

I moaned as I watched him, loving the passion he was showing. Cameron never showed the same enthusiasm, even when we were happy.

He lowered my leg then gripped my thong as he pulled it down my legs. I lifted my hips to help him get them off. Then he tossed them aside as he stared at the area between my legs. "I've wanted to do this for a long time." He moved his hands under my ass then dragged me to the end of the bed. Then he moved my legs back as he moved his face to the apex of my thighs. Then he kissed me with deliberate pressure, making me writhe on the bed instantly.

Jett circled my clitoris with his tongue then plunged deep inside me. He licked me savagely, like he needed me to keep going. He sucked hard then rubbed my clitoris with his thumb.

That made my body want to come. I clinched the sheets around me, and my head rolled back. "Jett...right there."

He quickly pulled away, his lips shiny from the wetness between my legs. "I want you to come when I'm inside you."

I growled because I couldn't wait that long. I sat up and yanked his shirt over his head.

"Someone's horny for me," he said like an arrogant jerk.

"Yeah, I am," I said bluntly. I got his jeans off then pulled down his boxers. When his long cock was revealed, I accidentally blurted, "Whoa."

That smug grin stretched a million times wider. "You think you can handle him, sweetheart?"

"Now I know why you're so cocky all the time—no pun intended."

"I'm a real man—unlike all those other boys out there."

I gripped his hips and pulled him closer to me while I sat at the edge of the bed. "Shut up. You're annoying."

His eyes darkened as he watched the tip of his cock come close to my mouth.

I gripped the base then licked the tip.

He took a deep breath. "Baby, you're fucking good at that."

I sucked him then deep-throated him as far as I could. My gag reflex wanted to go off but I fought it.

"Whoa...you don't have to prove anything to me." He gripped my neck and rocked his hips as he moved into my mouth. But he didn't move fast. Otherwise he might choke me. "Fuck, that feels good."

I pulled him out so I could get some air and sucked his tip. Then I took him far into my throat again.

His head rolled back and he groaned in pleasure. "Sweetheart, that feels fucking amazing but I'm not going to last much longer if you keep proving how well you can suck big dick."

I pulled him out then pressed a gentle kiss to his head. "As long as I made my point."

"You did—a million times over." He wrapped one arm around my waist then scooted me up the bed as he remained over me. "You have no idea how many times I've fantasized about this moment."

"That's pretty hot."

"Did you ever touch yourself and think about me?" He pressed his forehead to mine as his hands moved between my legs and he inserted two fingers inside me, making sure I was ready.

"Would you judge me if I said yes?"

"Not at all." He pulled his fingers out then licked them. "You're fucking soaked."

"I wonder why." I grabbed his shaft and gave him long, even strokes.

His breathing increased and he opened his nightstand to grab a condom. When he had it, he ripped it open with his teeth.

I snatched it then threw it on the ground. "I'm on the pill."

"Oh, thank god," he said blurted. "I fucking hate condoms." He moved my legs over his shoulders then leaned over me. Our bodies were pressed tightly together. I was pinned on the bed and his face was pressed to mine.

I hated condoms too. And I didn't want to wear one with a man I was monogamous with.

He directed his head at my entrance then slid inside. He took it slow because my body had to stretch for him. But the stretch felt so good. I'd never felt so full. I didn't think my body could handle him if he was any bigger.

"You doing okay, sweetheart?"

My fingers dug into his hair. "Oh yeah…"

He kept moving until he was completely inside me. "Holy shit, you're tight."

"You just have a big dick, Jett."

He didn't laugh or seem amused. His eyes were covered in a haze. He rocked into me slowly, his face pressed close to mine. He kissed me as he dug one hand into my hair.

Every time he moved into me it felt amazing. I groaned as he thrust into me, giving me all of him every time. "Jett…"

"I love it when you say my name, sweetheart." He breathed hard as he moved into me but he remained gentle, touching me delicately.

My hands moved into his hair while I looked him in the eye. "I love you." I felt the words burn in my heart and stretched to the rest of my body. He was my best friend and the person I trusted more than anyone else. What we had was special and different. And it may not have happened if we met under a different circumstance.

"I love you, sweetheart."

Our lovemaking was just like my dream. He touched me like he loved me, not needing to say the words to prove it, and judging the way he held me I knew he would never hurt me. We were two pieces of the same soul, two branches from the same tree.

He moved into me harder than rocked his body so he rubbed against my clitoris as he did it. "I'm going to make you come. If you scream, my landlord will kick me out. But I really don't care."

I was never a screamer but as I felt the sensation burn deep inside me I realized how wrong I was. My nails moved to his back and I held on as the explosion shattered me. "Jett…Jett…"

He slammed into me harder and made the pleasure last as long as possible. "You're beautiful when you come."

"Because I'm saying your name."

"That might have something to do with it." He brushed his lips passed mine then kissed my forehead. "Can I come inside you?"

"Please do." I grabbed his hips and used them to rock into him from below. I sheathed him over and over, doing most of the work. I wanted to make him feel as good as he made me feel.

"Fuck…" He tensed under my grasp and released a loud moan as he exploded. He sheathed himself completely as he came, filling me with his hot seed. I could feel the warmth deep inside me.

He stayed on top of me long after he finished, recovering from the pleasure we both felt. "This is mine." He moved his hips, his semi-hard dick sliding inside me.

"And this is mine." I grabbed his ass and pulled him into me.

"I'm glad we got that straightened out." Without pulling out of me, he moved to his side and took me with him. He pulled me tight against his body then hooked my legs around his waist. "Sleep with me every night—for at least two weeks."

"I'll clear my schedule."
"Or forever—whatever one you prefer."

E. L. Todd

epilogue

Jett

"Now look who's a pussy." Troy laughed before he took a drink. "You're whipped harder than all of us combined."

I shrugged in guilt. "I like being whipped."

"You're a sucker just like the rest of us," Rhett noted.

"Are we done with this now?" I asked.

"Nope," Cato said. "You teased me mercilessly. It's payback time, bitch."

All the guys laughed.

"You'll be next, River," Troy said. "Just wait and see."

River drank his beer. "I hope so. It's ironic, isn't it? I'm the only one who's actually wanted to settle down but I haven't."

"You'll find her," Rhett said. "She's just around the corner somewhere."

"I don't know," River said. "Maybe she'll turn up when I stop looking for her. That seems to be what happened to you clowns."

"You can give it a shot," I said.

"So, when's she going to be here?" Cato asked as he looked at his watch.

"She just got off work so she'll be here soon." The guys hadn't met Ophelia and they hadn't really seen her. They caught a glimpse of her in the bar when she caught Cameron cheating on her. But it was dark and everything happened so fast.

"I wonder if she's really as hot as you say," River said.

"She is," I said. "But you better not say it. I'll have to kill you."

River laughed and rolled his eyes at the same time.

The door to the bar opened and a pretty brunette walked inside. She wore a champagne pink dress with a black cardigan. Black stilettos were on her feet and her hair was in a high, slick ponytail.

"There she is," I said.

All the guys turned.

"Don't make it obvious!"

"Too late." River sipped his beer while he stared at her legs.

I growled then slid out of the booth.

Ophelia spotted me then smiled. Then she came my way.

I loved it when she smiled at me. It was the most beautiful thing in the world. "Hey, sweetheart. How was work?"

"Terrible because I was away from you." She wrapped her arms around my neck and gave me a kiss.

I pulled her flush against my chest and kissed her hard. I wanted to devour her right then and there.

Ophelia pulled away then noticed the guys staring at her. "Uh…hi."

"Can you stop gawking at my girlfriend?" I said with a growl.

The guys pretended they weren't starting.

"Ophelia, these are the guys. Guys, this is Ophelia."

She smiled then shook hands with each of them. "It's nice to meet you."

"You got a sister?" River asked.

"A gay brother," she said.

"Well, if he's as hot as you I might give it a shot."

I shot River a glare.

"What?" he asked in innocence. "You kept saying how hot she was. Of course I'm going to check her out."

Ophelia blushed and smiled at the same time.

At least she was a good sport about it. "I'm sorry about them."

"It's okay," she said. "They're cute."

"Cute?" I asked.

River smiled. "You hear that, boys? She thinks we're cute."

"Well, we are," Troy said. "Look at us."

"Now I know where you get your cockiness from," Ophelia noted.

"No, I get my cockiness from my dick. You know that too well."

She smacked my arm playfully.

"Can I get you a drink?" I asked.

"A beer is fine."

"Coming right up. Take a seat." I headed to the bar then got her something on tap. When I returned to the table River had his arm around her and he was talking to her in a deep conversation.

"If we could make a computer that could download our memories and thoughts, we could live forever as a machine," River said. "Wouldn't that be amazing?"

"It would," she agreed.

"Okay…enough of that." I pushed his arm off her then placed mine instead.

"I was just making sure no one snatched her while you were gone," River said with a wink.

"I'm sure," I said sarcastically.

"So, are you a model?" Troy blurted.

"No," Ophelia said quietly. "I work in fashion."

"She's a chief editor," I said proudly. "She's smart, she's cute, and she's got style."

Ophelia gave me a quick smile.

"And she's got a tight pussy, apparently," Cato said.

I shot him a glare. Of course I told my boys about the sex. But they weren't supposed to mention it.

"But that's a really important quality," Ophelia said as she played along.

I shot her a smile. "I'm glad you agree."

"Jett's favorite thing to do is kiss. He's says it's better and more intimate than sex." She shot me a victorious look.

"Really?" Troy turned to me. "You really are a pussy."

"Payback is a bitch, huh?" Ophelia said with a smirk.

I rubbed my nose against hers. "I guess we're even."

"So, I've always wanted to know this," Cato said. "Is he really gay? Because when he was pretending to be gay he was pretty convincing…"

"Shut up, asshole." I kicked him under the table.

"He fooled me," she said. "Especially when I changed in front of him in the dressing room."

River chuckled. "What a dog."

"He really was," Ophelia agreed.

"You really can't blame me," I said. "With an ass like that what am I supposed to do? Close my eyes?"

"Yes," she said. "That's exactly what you should have done."

"Then I really would have been a pussy, "I said.

"Like you aren't now," she jabbed.

River laughed. "I like her. She's like one of the guys."

"You did good." Troy clanked his beer against mine.

"I'll drink to that." Rhett moved his glass in, and soon we were all joining in.

Then I turned to Ophelia. "I think you're in."

"You were stuck with me whether I was or not." She gave me a playful look before she kissed me sensually.

My hand moved to her thigh and I kissed her harder, wishing we were home.

"Okay, enough of that," Rhett said.

"Like you aren't jerking off under the table," Troy said.

"I am," River said. "I'm not ashamed."

I continued to kiss her, knowing I'd found the woman to share my life with. We didn't find each other in a traditional way, but that didn't decrease the love we had for each other.

Actually, it made it stronger.

book five of the beautiful entourage series

seductive GUEST

River & Meadow

AVAILABLE NOW

Show Your Support

Like E. L. Todd on Facebook:

https://www.facebook.com/ELTodd42?ref=hl

Follow E. L. Todd on Twitter:

@E_L_Todd

Subscribe to E. L. Todd's Newsletter:

www.eltoddbooks.com

Other Books by E. L. TODD

Alpha Series

Sadie

Elisa

Layla

Janet

Cassie

Hawaiian Crush Series

Connected By The Sea

Breaking Through The Waves

Connected By The Tide

Taking The Plunge

Riding The Surf

Laying in the Sand

Forever and Always Series

Only For You

Forever and Always

Edge of Love

E. L. Todd

Force of Love

Fight For Love

Lover's Roulette

Happily Ever After

The Wandering Caravan

Come What May

Again and Again

Lover's Road

Meant To Be

Here and Now

Until Forever

New Beginnings

Love Conquers All

Love Hurts

The Last Time

Sweet Sins

Lost in Time

Closing Time

Southern Love

Then Came Alexandra

Then Came Indecision

Then Came Absolution

Then Came Abby

Abby's Plight

Printed in Great Britain
by Amazon